57kction

mourning
CRAZY
HORSE

mourning CRAZY HORSE

stories by
HAROLD JAFFE

FICTION COLLECTIVE

Copyright © 1982 by Harold Jaffe
All rights reserved.

First Edition

LCCN: 81-71645
ISBN 0-914590-72-3
ISBN 0-914590-73-1 (paper)

Many of these stories were published in *fiction international, Aspect, The Minnesota Review, Fiction, Chicago Review, O.ARS,* and *New Directions in Prose and Poetry.*

Grateful acknowledgement is made to the following for permission to quote or paraphrase brief passages: Gaston Bachelard, *The Poetics of Space* (Boston: Beacon Press, 1969); John Blofeld, *Taoism, The Road to Immortality* (Boulder: Shambhala, 1978); John Bierhorst, ed.: *In the Trail of the Wind: American Indian Poems and Ritual Orations* (New York: Farrar, Straus and Giroux, 1971); Noam Chomsky, Introduction to Daniel Guérin's *Anarchism* (New York: Monthly Review Press, 1970); R.T. Rundle Clark, *Myth and Symbol in Ancient Egypt* (London: Thames and Hudson, 1959); Graham Greene, *England Made Me* (New York: Penguin, 1945); Hans Hess, *George Grosz* (New York: Macmillan, 1974); Barry Holstun Lopez, *Of Wolves and Men* (New York: Scribner's, 1978); Paul Radin, *The Trickster: A Study in American Indian Mythology* (New York: Schocken Books, 1972); F.W. Turner, ed.: *The Portable North American Indian Reader* (New York: Viking, 1974); *Twenty-Five German Poets, a Bilingual Collection,* Ed., Translated and Introduced by Walter Kaufmann, W.W. Norton & Co., Inc. Copyright © 1975 by Walter Kaufmann. Copyright © 1962 by Random House, Inc. The lines from "To Those Born After," by Brecht, are reprinted with the permission of W.W. Norton.

I am grateful, also, to Howard Sann for editorial suggestions.

The publication of this book is in part made possible with support from the National Endowment for the Arts and the New York State Council on the Arts.

Typeset by Open Studio in Rhinebeck, N.Y., a non-profit facility for writers, artists and independent literary publishers, supported in part by grants from the New York State Council on the Arts and the National Endowment for the Arts.

Published by Fiction Collective with assistance from the National Endowment for the Arts and New York State Council on the Arts.

for my red sister
my black brother

CONTENTS

PART I

PART II

PART I

you cannot harm me
you cannot harm
one who has dreamed
a dream like mine

(Ojibwa)

SWEDE

SWEDE

A large man with rigid broad shoulders, his long back held straight and somewhat stiff. The exercise trunks worn high, above the navel. The legs long, well-developed, hairless. The surprisingly slender ankles sockless in old-fashioned black and white high-top sneakers. The face pink, rather broad, even-featured, not without refinement. But the thinnish lips pressed together irritably, and the grey eyes vexed, pained...

The man was obviously a Swede, Rosen called him Nillson. They met in the exercise room of the Mid-Manhattan YMCA. "Met" isn't accurate; Rosen saw Nillson, observed him, extrapolated certain crucial data from his appearance, gestures, his encounters with the other exercisers. Of this last there was almost none: Carlito, a Puerto Rican of chronic cheer, grinned and exchanged a word or two with Nillson. Supine, side-by-side on their sit-up boards, Carlito might utter something loudly about the weather, and after a pause Nillson would briefly nod his head, or even venture something in return, softly, his lips scarcely moving, wishing neither his few words nor, particularly, the timbre of his voice to be overheard.

Among the data Rosen accumulated was that Nillson had been in the U.S. for about a decade, that he was unmarried, that he lived alone in a small and depressing flat on the West Side, that his isolation and anger were in the process of unbalancing him.

Rosen of course could not speak with him. Nor had their eyes ever met. Once Nillson was doing bench-presses with rather heavy weight, and after the fourth or fifth repetition became stuck with the large barbell on his chest. This happened on occasion to others, and always the person stuck would call out for someone to remove the weight. Nillson didn't call out. On his back on the narrow bench he struggled silently to push the weight from his chest. His face reddened violently, the tendons in his neck stiffened and swelled; with his utmost effort he could lift the barbell five or six inches off his chest, no more...

Rosen didn't intervene, not yet.

...It continued, and though there were ten or a dozen other exercisers in the wide room, only Rosen witnessed the Swede's silent, losing battle. Short of someone intervening, the Swede had but a single recourse, somewhat dangerous and very noisy. It was to tilt the bar either left or right so that the plates (which were slipped, not fastened, onto the bar) would crash to the floor. Immediately of course the lopsided end would tilt perilously and perhaps crash into Nillson's body.

Nillson didn't do this, not wanting to call attention to himself. Rosen came to his aid, helped lift the bar from his chest and set it on the rack above his head. Nillson, still very red, was breathing hard; Rosen standing above him, one hand on the bar which rested on the rack.

"Thanks," Nillson said finally, softly, in a slight accent, still on his back, not looking at his intercessor.

"Sure," Rosen said. He moved away.

When Rosen saw him again nearly a week later, the Swede did not greet him. He moved from the sit-up board to the dumbbell rack, to the chinning-bar where he did four chins, then hung to stretch his vertebrae, to the bench-press station where he did five repetitions— with moderate weight. Between exercises Nillson leaned his right shoulder against a wall and read the *Times*. When he was finished in the exercise room he went upstairs to the steam room. Here he sat on the tile bench with a towel draped about his waist and his head in his hands. After fifteen minutes or so in the steam room, he showered. Then, with the towel tied about his waist, he went downstairs to the locker room. He wore shower shoes and walked deliberately with long strides.

It was a fortnight to the day after the bench-press incident that Rosen waited for the Swede in the YMCA lobby, and proceeded to follow him. The Swede had completed his workout and walked down the stairs (instead of riding the elevator as nearly everyone else did). Nillson carried an old black briefcase in which he transported his soiled and wet gym clothes. Possibly he carried other things in the briefcase as well; Rosen rather suspected he did, though he couldn't imagine what.

A few minutes past three, early Fall, it had just stopped raining. Nillson wore a white wash-and-wear short-sleeved shirt, tieless but buttoned at the throat, khaki poplin trousers (cuffed, evidently part of a suit), and, oddly, the same high-top sneakers he wore in the exercise room. His thinning, fine-spun, grey-blond hair was mussed, still damp from the shower. Striding fairly rapidly, Nillson turned north at the corner and commenced to make his way uptown. His left arm he swung back and forth stiffly in a faintly jerky martial-like rhythm. His right hand, holding the briefcase, he kept stiff at his side. Short-legged Rosen shadowed the bemused Swede at fifteen meters.

Nillson had walked north to 37th Street, his head stiff and straight and higher than nearly everyone he passed, crossing at the green lights, managing to squeeze across at the red, only once pausing. At 37th a bus and a taxi had gotten into a small accident, and as the two drivers screamed at each other within a small circle in the street, bystanders clustered at the scene with amused, cynical expressions on their faces. No room to cross here—the Swede, uninterested in the accident, cut east to Fifth, and then to Madison. At Madison he turned north again. He didn't glance at shop windows, nor did he seem to observe the attractive women, and yet his stride was not so much purposeful as... compelled. Or so it seemed.

Finally he did pause on Madison and 48th, at a sweet shop. He entered, purchased a bar of Swiss chocolate, opened the wrapper in the shop and ate the chocolate as he continued uptown at the same pace, in the same rhythm, except that every fifteenth step or so his piston-like left hand lifted higher, depositing another small panel of chocolate in his jaws.

At Madison and 56th another small crowd had assembled; in its midst stood a slim woman with a *noli-me-tangere* expression on her adolescent features. It was Jacqueline Onassis who had just stepped out of a cab. Her minuscule breasts were naked, Rosen supposed, beneath her dress and fur. The Swede either didn't recognize her or didn't care; he veered sharply east to Park, he bit into his chocolate, he turned north.

Tall rectangular structures of glass and steel entrenched Park Avenue to the east and west. These were banks and "trusts." Above the sparkling lobbies and mezzanines, the managers resided with their families and Swiss timepieces and small dogs. An occasional flat on a lower floor was reserved for a proctologist or psychoanalyst. Nillson, striding solemnly, moved through the tunnel-like thoroughfare, the briefcase held stiffly in his right hand, the other hand propelling him onward with short rhythmic jabs. He had finished his chocolate and stuffed the wrapper in the left front pocket of his trousers. It was fifteen minutes in front of four...

It was becoming overcast. At 85th and Park a funeral procession intercepted the Swede's angle. A hearse followed by a cortège of long cars with their headlights on coursed slowly from west to east. Nillson waited. Then — unexpectedly — he lowered himself to the pavement and opened his briefcase. He withdrew a large brown envelope which he undid, withdrawing from it...something. Rosen, ten meters behind, his curved back pressed to the angular glass revolving door of a New York Savings and Trust, dared not move closer. The funeral procession coursed silently, lengthily, a peculiar snake, from west to east. Nillson on one knee appeared to be sorting or shuffling the contents of the large envelope. Rosen seized his chance and stole forward...but now the funeral procession had passed, Nillson had replaced the envelope in his briefcase and was striding northward.

At 94th and Park Rosen felt drizzle, a drop on his head, another on his nose. Meanwhile Nillson had cut east again: to Lexington, and then farther east to Third. At Third Avenue he continued north. 97th Street represented the unofficial southernmost frontier of Harlem; Nillson had just passed 98th without the slightest diminuendo in his pace. The change was gradual for a street or two: a dusky face in a car, in front of a building...then it was total: the stiff-shouldered, pink-skinned Swede and the ambiguous though indisputably caucasian Rosen behind him at fifteen paces — were pigmentless in Harlem.

At 103rd Street the occasional amused and ironic stares began. Comments:

"Where they think they at?"

"Hey, long pink bro."

"Faggots..."

"What the dwarf up to?"

This last referred to Rosen, who wasn't precisely afraid. Nor was he offended, since the brothers had no way of knowing who he was.

Nillson, striding jerkily forward, heard nothing, saw little. It was five before five, the drizzle had now become rain, steady and heavy. Rosen fastened a handkerchief about his mouth. They were at 112th Street, the normally congested streets had thinned out. Rain or no, it was Harlem: wounded, flailing even, yet vital as ever. (Rosen knew Harlem.) It was raining harder. The Swede was soaked through, his shirt and trousers clinging wetly to his body, his old briefcase drenched, creaturely in his right fist. The streets had emptied.

125th Street cut like a neon spine through Harlem's trunk. Nillson strode past it, at 127th he turned east to Second Avenue, then north again. Rosen had a feeling they were coming close—he didn't know to what. It wouldn't be good.

At 132nd Street a "gypsy" cab driver speeding north screeched noisily to a halt between Rosen and the Swede and began to honk his horn.

"Hey, brother dwarf, take a ride, yawl gonna drown if you don."

As the cab driver was shouting Nillson actually paused and turned his head. He saw Rosen and possibly even recognized him. Rosen thought he observed something like recognition in the Swede's sopping face. But then he was moving again, faster than before, crossing the street, striding down 133rd to the East River Drive. Rosen hung back for several seconds, then made after him at about twenty meters. The gypsy cab driver drove alongside still trying to coax a fare.

"Howsabout it, brother dwarf, I give you a good price..."

Rosen scarcely heard these words, pushing as he was with some urgency after Nillson. The pelting rain made it difficult to see, and by the time Rosen had sloshed his way to the East River Drive he had lost the Swede, didn't see him anywhere.

"Yo! brother dwarf." It was the gypsy cab driver—he had reached the Drive before Rosen.

"Yawl lookin for that stiff big dude?"

"You saw him?"

"He went into that building there. Facin the river."

An old five or six storey tenement tottered next to a river warehouse on the east side of the wide street. The ground floor had contained a small luncheonette, partially boarded over and long obsolete according to the scrawled prices of hot plates and sandwiches still visible in the window.

Rosen pushed open the sluggish cast iron door, entered the narrow corridor and commenced to climb the steep wooden stairs. Very damp, smelling of must and decay, also the faint salt smell of the river; rain clattering on the roof, against the walls. It occurred to Rosen that the gypsy cab driver might have been jiving him. He had not seen a mailbox; obviously the building was unlived in. Rosen, though, believed him, believed that the Swede *had* entered this building, was somewhere within it.

On the first landing were two doors, but both had been boarded up long ago by the look of the wood and the nails. The corridor was of course dark; Rosen made his examination with a small Japanese flashlight he carried on his person.

While proceeding up to the next landing he heard something high above him, as though a heavy door were being dislodged. It would be the roof. As Rosen made his way rapidly upstairs he saw the rain streaming into the building and down the stairwell. Breathing heavily Rosen mounted the last flight, saw the iron ladder at once and climbed up and through the opening where the steel roof panel was dislodged.

With his head and torso on the roof Rosen shined his light; thick pelting rain, cloudy dark—he could see almost nothing. He pushed himself onto the roof and moved ahead cautiously—the roof slanted, the footing was slick. He was shining his light on the street side when he heard something from the river side: at once he turned his light in the direction of the sound and saw a figure—the Swede—glaring at him with intense expressionless eyes, moving back away from him— and off the roof! Seconds later Rosen heard an indefinite plash—or thought he did. The rain was making such a clatter. Rosen crawled to the edge of the roof on hands and knees...close to the edge his right hand brushed something wet, animal. He recoiled, then shined his light: the Swede's sopping briefcase. Rosen took hold of it, then extended himself onto his belly and peered over. The river was making a din, along with the rain; about all he could determine was that with a slight propulsion it was possible to go from roof to river. Nillson...

Rosen fitted the heavy steel panel into place behind him and descended the ladder. The first sound he had heard while on the roof must have been Nillson dropping his briefcase. That would have to be it. As Rosen was about to make his way downstairs he observed that one of the two doors on the top-most landing, the door farther from the roof opening, was slightly ajar. He pushed it open with his foot and, after a slight pause, went inside. It appeared to be a flat of three or four rooms—the shell of a flat, nothing was there, the ceiling and walls were crumbling, electric wires snaked from exposed outlets in the ceilings and baseboards. Rosen moved into another room, then a third which apparently had been the kitchen. Here only the old-fashioned potbelly sink was still intact. As Rosen moved toward the sink he kicked something, picked it up—a small metal canister, empty. It had contained film, and from the looks of it had been recently used. Shining his light in the sink itself Rosen saw that a pan had been fitted into it—and then he became aware of a faint vinegary odor. Developing solution? Yes, there was some still in the pan. The sink had been transformed into a kind of dark room.

Rosen remembered the briefcase. He had set it down someplace when he entered the flat. It was near the door, he opened it. Nillson's gym clothes were within, waterlogged. In another section was the large brown envelope. Opening this he found...photographs. They too had gotten wet, were stuck together. Carefully Rosen separated them; there must have been at least two dozen, all positives, all— Rosen was shining the light—of Nillson. In most of them he was naked, standing, framed by a crumbling wall or grimy window...

(One knee on the splintery wood floor, the sopping dwarfish man examined the snapshots of the naked—now dead—Swede.)

...Nillson himself must have taken the photos, and in that very flat—the windows and walls were unmistakable. The naked photos were almost without variation: Nillson standing, facing the camera, with his arms held stiffly by his sides. In a few a glimmer of river was dimly visible beyond the window. The Swede looked quite like himself: pink, stiff, large, though his genitals, flaccid in each photograph, were unexceptional, neither large nor small.

The other photos were posed in the same way, except that Nillson was clothed and in some of these had his hands folded across his groin rather than at his sides. Invariable in every photograph was the expression: intense, vexed, isolated. *More* than isolated...

Rosen, exceptionally alert, inspecting minutely with his small light, saw now keenly what had been merely suggested before: a frozen vacuity about the Swede's matte-like features, as if a part of him was already pledged to the other side.

MOURNING
CRAZY HORSE

(for R.W.)

MOURNING CRAZY HORSE

5 September 1877. Crazy Horse gone. Shoshone, Oglala, Lakota, Brulé.

I stand on the canyon floor in northeast Arizona looking up at the Anasazi petroglyph on the cliff wall: a humpbacked shaman dancing, playing a wooden flute. From Arizona I mean to head north.

When Dull Knife came with his starving Shyelas, Crazy Horse saw how it was. He left camp and went into the hills where squatting in the cold he fasted and dreamed. It was in a dream when he was a boy that he had seen his pony dance and had received his name. That was not so long ago, but it was a different time.

In Black Hat, New Mexico I stop for a drink in the only air conditioned bar on the strip, the Holiday Inn. A young white man sitting next to me on his leatherette stool says that his name is Duane and begins to talk. He's out of work, nearly out of money, he's planning on going to Albuquerque to join a friend who bought a share in a Texaco service station franchise, he thinks he can get work there; "I'd better," he says, "if I don't, I don't know..." As he talks I hear the electronic whine and click and whistle of a pinball machine in the corridor. When I came in I noticed two boys five or six years younger than Duane at the machine. The waitress who delivers my beer in a frosted mug is trussed up in a kind of bunny costume, her thirtyish face tired and resigned, flaccid buttocks jiggling as she transports my dollar-fifty to the cash register. Beyond the murmur of the bar and pinball I can hear the eighteen wheel semis revving up outside near the truckstop diner.

Crazy Horse's skin was oddly white for a Sioux. Or so it was said. He never permitted his "shadow to be caught" in a photograph. In Black Elk's account,

Crazy Horse was thirty years old when he was murdered. Betrayed by Little Big Man. Crazy Horse's mother and father fastened up a pony drag and carried away their son's corpse (some said it was his heart which they had cut away from the corpse). None of the mourners followed them. It is said that they buried Crazy Horse in Wounded Knee Creek.

The neon sign atop the motel read: U TIRED
                                      HAVE REST
                                      KLIN UNITS

This is just south of Mt. Zion National Park in southern Utah. My room contains a color TV but only a 25 watt bulb in the reading lamp by the bed. The family in the adjoining unit keeps their tape recorder going in their pickup as they unload their luggage. I hear a country and western tune called "Lonesome, Ornery and Mean" by a male vocalist, and two or three other tunes by a female with an affected vibrato. I lie on my back on the narrow bed and leaf through a magazine I picked up at a truckstop diner on the freeway...

The "Agency" wanted the Black Hills and finally they got what they wanted. They didn't want the Black Hills until the yellow metal that drives whiteskins crazy was discovered there. Then they wanted the hills very bad, and after many battles and other kinds of persuasion that they are expert at, they managed to get three or four chiefs to scratch their signatures on a long sheet of paper. After the Agency took the Black Hills Crazy Horse's dreams became deeper and longer-lasting than before. And the more immersed Crazy Horse became in his dreaming the more he gave away: bridle, headdress, blanket...Gifts to his people.

Called HIGHWAY EVANGELIST, the magazine contains millenarian quotations from the New Testament, as well as letters from readers, including this one:

Dear HIGHWAY EVANGELIST,

Have read a couple of yr issues and enjoyed them. Must tell you I love all those 18 wheelers. They fascinate me. If I was abt 25 yrs younger, wd sure like to drive one. But at 61, that's a little too old for that. So my wish now is to ride in one. Also wd like to make a collection of photos of 18 wheelers and drivers for a short history of each one. I sit at my window in the evenings and watch those big rigs go by. I know lots of the drivers from the Dakotas as I get to talk to them on my CB.

In town we have a diner where they stop to eat. I get to meet them and talk to them and some I know by name. It's real interesting listening to them. These men are a very special breed. Christ has to be with them. I say a little prayer for them all.

A nice trucker helped me one day when I had a blowout on I-90. He was from PA. Ever since we have been good CB buddies. He comes to Fargo abt once a month. My CB handle is Indian Lady.

Thanks for letting me bend yr ear. If any tucker wd like to send me a photo of himself and his rig, wd love to have them.

Christ bless them all.

> Hilde Wolcott
> Box 352
> Fargo, N.D. 04421

The available data, most of which are derived from oral sources, confirm that Crazy Horse was unsurpassed both as warrior and dreamer, that he was as unfailingly generous to his people as he was implacable to their oppressor. He was slight of build, with faded skin, and no one was considered stranger, more impenetrable. But his was the strangeness of genius, of sanctity. Or so the records indicate. His single child, a daughter, born to his wife Black Shawl, he named They Are Afraid Of Her. She died before her fifth year of the choking cough transmitted by the white trader's sons. Crazy Horse was murdered in his thirtieth year, in the Moon When The Calf Grows Hair.

After passing through Shining Mountain and over Mad River I find myself in a "family restaurant" in Orem, Utah, ordering the overpriced special. Into my skull leaps the wild sentence I read in one of the Mormon pamphlets left in my motel room the evening before: "One year ago I received the gift of cancer."

Crazy Horse could not read, knew nothing of "world affairs," refused to be photographed, wore the "ghost shirt" but would not dance as the others did. When he led his braves into battle against the bluecoats he had them fight to kill and not to "count coups" or take trophy scalps.

Avoiding the reservations, I drove from Oklahoma to Texas to New Mexico to Arizona to Nevada to Utah to Idaho to Montana to North Dakota...Aside from the sixteen year old Navaho boy who acted as my guide in Canyon de Chelly National Monument in northeastern Arizona, the only two other Indians I saw were in Las Rosas, New Mexico and Clinton, Oklahoma, both drunk, one slumped on his spine against a railroad trestle, the other staggering back and forth on the strip asking for handouts. Possibly one other: a languid, prettyfaced adolescent in a truckstop diner near Amarillo. He was dressed like a cowboy, his white stetson tipped back on his thick purple hair, an indolent dreamy look in his black eyes as he played one cowboy ballad after another on the jukebox.

When the warriors braided their ponies' tails and then painted their faces for war, the women made the tremolo in their rejoicing that their men would be killing the enemy. The braves meanwhile gave up their passion for their women, it being best that a warrior unsex himself, that he carry his grievance like a cold weight in his stomach. The sacred stone which Crazy Horse carried and which grew heavy in times of danger, had grown so heavy that his pony gave out. Worm gave Crazy Horse his own pony, a buckskin mare, her tail braided for war. This was before the battle in the valley of Rosebud where Crazy Horse led his braves to a victory over Three Star Crook and his column of bluecoats.

I exit the freeway at Rosebud, Montana. One of the guidebooks mentioned the Rosebud Museum. On the strip the Exxon attendant's deadpan creases into a vague glimmer of recognition after half a minute. "Take a right past the railroad tracks, follow the tracks for about a mile, mile and a half. You can't miss it."

Shoshone, Oglala, Lakota, Brulé.

I walk past the weeping birches and horse chestnut trees up the stone steps into the cavernous Greek Revival structure. The difficult-to-define, but unmistakable, odor of chronic senseless busy-work informs me that I am in the wrong place. I ask a janitor who points across the green to a narrow quonset hut-like building...A blonde young woman raises her head as I enter. The Rosebud Museum contains memorabilia from the years of the first white settlement to the present: photos and menus belonging to a gaggle of wives who called themselves the "Rosebud Cowbelles," old saddles and water mills and prairie schooner fixtures, several photos of the Rosebud Little League baseball team whose uniforms were "donated by the Rosebud chapter of the VFW." The young blonde, in tight faded jeans and a brief cotton top, leads me around, managing often to bend, her tiny convex navel exposed like a pink peculiar genital, as she presses against this or that dusty display case.

Moon Of The Dark Red Calf, 1877. Crazy Horse was spending most of his time dreaming and lamenting in the hills above the camp. It was said that he had unbraided his pony's tail and was through with fighting. But when his warriors showed their sadness, he joked with them, told them that the fighting was far from over. But it was bad. We all knew that it was bad.

In Medora, North Dakota, I drive into Theodore Roosevelt National Park, 70,000 acres of "badlands." Roosevelt hunted and ranched in these badlands in the 1880's and "fell in love with the plateaus and buttes and conical hills, with the many weird and brilliantly colored formations." When he took up residence in Washington he donated his ranchland to the national weal; this in effect was the beginning of our national park system. And this park "pays tribute to the contributions made by Teddy Roosevelt toward the conservation of our country's natural resources." So the plaque in the visitor center explains. I purchase a field guide to local flora, pay the park ranger at the desk, get into my car, turn around and drive back out onto the freeway.

In the Spring of 1877 Crazy Horse was told that the Great Father wanted him and the other big chiefs of the Sioux nation to travel to Washington to confer with him. This was in the Moon Of The Grass Appearing. Crazy Horse declined to go. Also at about this time Crazy Horse learned that Three Star Crook was bribing Sioux warriors to help him fight the Nez Perces who were still holding out against the bluecoats in the northwest. It pained Crazy Horse to hear this and he spoke out strongly against it in the sweat lodges, at the ghost dance gatherings, wherever he had access to the chiefs and elders.

Autumn, 1980. Our sweetest outlaws are barechested, wear stetsons, have a marketable patois, are reassuringly white-skinned, tattoo their rigs with Country, Playboy and Jesse James Christ, push their rigs to 80 on a downgrade, refuse to relinquish the passing lane on an upgrade, are the subjects of song, cinema and beer commercials... The railroad, like a household negro, shuffles from one dusty corner to another humming an old church tune.

Three Star Crook got wind of Crazy Horse's seditious counsels. He dispatched four companies of soldiers to "escort" Crazy Horse to Fort Robinson where, according to Three Star, the two of them would decide how best to remove the remaining Sioux to reservation land set aside for them near the Powder River. Crazy Horse, who had been fasting and dreaming for several consecutive days, had himself reluctantly concluded that the prospects of his people were at present without hope. After sending his braves away from camp into the hills, Crazy Horse awaited the soldiers.

Even on the freeway, driving east through Dakota, one feels the badlands, more implacable in their way than the Amazonian jungle, resisting (as the jungles have been unable to resist) "development." They seep, these badlands, into the veins, like the residue of a crucial childhood dream, all unremembered but the texture, a fragment of texture... Coffee seeps. White-recorded history must not seep.

Once in Fort Robinson Crazy Horse was taken to a Major Lee, who while remaining seated behind his desk said only that it was now too late for talking. Instead Crazy Horse was placed under arrest and led away by two guards, one a whiteskin officer, the other Little Big Man. The same Little Big Man who had said many times that he would joyfully die fighting rather than turn the Black Hills over to the Agency, was now an Agency Policeman. Little Big Man actually spoke some words into Crazy Horse's ears, but they went unheard.

Still in the badlands, stopping at a "scenic overlook," I withdraw the fieldguide I bought in Roosevelt National Park and turn to a passage I underscored: "Certain of these species have a wild vitality, a kind of plant patience and persistence that has brought their kind through countless weather cycles and natural disasters. Most of them are profligate with seed…Some will lie dormant, awaiting a favorable season, for a century or even longer."

As they drew close to a wood and brick building Crazy Horse saw that the windows were barred with steel and that huddled within were braves, their legs and arms in irons. At once Crazy Horse lunged away, pulling a knife from his sash. But Little Big Man grabbed him from behind and while he held him that way a soldier bayoneted Crazy Horse in the stomach. The whiteskin soldier's name was William Gentles. It is not known whether Crazy Horse regained consciousness. He died that same night.

"…at daybreak I roam,
ready to tear up the world
I roam…"

THE BLOOD
DONOR

THE BLOOD DONOR

Even as he slept—alert to the harpist above him—August could feel in his stomach he was hating. When he awoke on the overcast March morning in his narrow room it was bad. He lay abed hearing the harpist above him, not strumming—she was rarely at her harp—but standing in front of her dresser appraising her bloodless face and shuffling her high-heeled feet. Something dropped rattling across the uncarpeted floor. Then her phone rang: she *ran* to answer it, puncturing August's skull with each stiletto-heeled jab.

This sequence—with one or two variants—initiated August's every day. When she wasn't heeled (rare), she treaded on the floor on her bare, broad feet.

All right: three salvos of high-strung laughter, an echoing high-pitched "goodbye," and phone call's over: *Bong!* phone deposited jarringly in its cradle, vile red-haired harpist clacking nervously back to her dresser...

August swore, climbed out of his bed, swore, pushed into the bathroom, dislodged some phlegm and spat into the basin. In the glare and buzz of his fluorescent shaving mirror he fitted (with trembling hands) the corrugated red-haired head atop his own mussed head and slit her throat with his Wilkinson steel razor. Her pale mucousy discharge smelled rancid, like standing urine.

After his shave (styptic! styptic!) and lead-off execution, August was straddling his alcove kitchen fussing with his coffee. His stomach hurt. Two months ago he went to a new physician for a "GI series." The result was negative, but his stomach still hurt, hurt more than before as he recalled now (his coffee not right, watery) how he had loathed the nurse at the front desk. Cerberus-like, she had intercepted him as he had entered the waiting-room and proceeded to grill him on his "medical history" loudly (the others in the waiting-room heard her every word) and in a most insolent manner, as if to say: "I couldn't care less about you or the piddling intimate details of your life. I do it because it is a disagreeable facet of my high-paying job."

August, standing, sipped his coffee loathing her airs, her contempt, her airy repudiation of him. Loathing her patchy armadillo's head (he recalled her aspect distinctly), August balanced it atop his own head—it felt an awful weight—lifted the just-boiled kettle from the stove and poured deliberately, scalding, dispatching the monstrous head.

Rosen the humpback repeated a sutra for August. Then he stepped out into the lurid sun. At 45th and 8th he adopted his street-wise shuffle and was immediately accosted.

"Hey, little rube, wanna stick your hump in my pocket?"

Rosen smiled. She had Rhonda Fleming's hair, wore puce hotpants, and smirked from her exposed navel. Rosen had begun to perspire above his upper lip. He gave her his gopher smile.

"Whatchoo frettin about, dwarf-guy?"

She was talking out at him from the storefront of a pornographic bookstore. Books, Magazines, "Sundries."

"How do you know I'm fretting?"

"It ain't hard to tell on you, Bo. You a feeling guy, ain't you?"

Rosen hesitated for just an instant, then said, "How about some coffee?"

She giggled. "Come closer, honey." She squatted on her stiletto heels, took hold of Rosen's large head and wriggled her tongue into his ear. "How about some wombat, dwarf-guy?"

Rosen was aware of her perfume. It was potent, floral. He recognized, he thought, the scent...

"What's your name?"

"Harriet."

"Well, you're right, Harriet. I'm fretting."

"I got just the thang." She patted her crotch.

Rosen had become aroused. But he said, "You don't understand. I'm not fretting about myself. His name is August."

"August?" She placed her hands on her hips and tilted her head. "You a faggot?"

Before Rosen could respond she said, "Don't get me wrong. I ain't got nothin against them. Faggots. Matter of fak I kinda almost..."

"What do you have in mind, Harriet?"

"C'mon up to my room, little stud. Cos you five fives, I'm gonna take your edge off real sweet, also make things real good for your buddy."

"Five fives?"

"Right. Ain't nothin cos what it use to. You come back in a month fum now ita cos you six fives. I know a special kind of voodoo. You ever hear of the magic bone?"

Rosen slid his tongue along his upper lip. "Magic bone?"

Subwaying to Wall, August wore his wombat. The chapped-lipped marsupial in the token booth at August's stop infuriated him with his cynical deliberateness even as the train—August's train—was hurtling into the station. Several times he had missed his train because of this cretin, and this morning it happened again. He set the wombat token-seller atop his hat. At 59th Street, where he changed for the Express, August waited until the door was just about to slide shut—then exited, all of him but the wombat, crisply guillotined by the peremptory door.

Behind Harriet, whose ass wealth and thigh swayed rhythmic as surf, Rosen mounted the noisome stairs up and up...

Harriet over her shoulder: "How do you feel about my puce hot-pants, brother dwarf?"

"I feel very—" Rosen paused, he was breathing thickly. "I feel very positive about them."

"I made them myself."

"I...see."

"Not yet, brother dwarf. You'll see soon. Your buddy too. What's he called again?"

"Au—" Rosen could hardly talk. "August. How much higher?"

Harriet laughed. "Next landing."

Pent August stepped into the elevator and waited. Others entered, one or two nodded to him. They carried attaché cases. He returned their brief nods. One said, "Morning, Augie."

"Morning," August said.

August was headless until the 28th floor. That was his floor, and when he emerged he was balancing atop his own sober snap-brim the penguiny head of his immediate superior, punctilious Scanlon out of Peekskill. Scanlon was of course already there. He glanced at his wristwatch as August, nodding good morning, made his way through the common room to his alcove office.

August appeared to be removing his snap-brim hat with both hands when Scanlon entered his alcove. In fact he was throttling the officious penguin even as he was being addressed by him.

"...those certificates completed by April one..."

August heard principally the final enforced breaths.

"Do you hear me, August?"

"April one," August repeated, setting the lifeless head on his desk, his first gargoyle paperweight of the Monday morning.

Harriet's narrow room with its single corner window was not unfamiliar. The window looked out on a narrow gutter across which stood an old oblong industrial building.

Grinning, her hands on her hips, Harriet observed Rosen's reconnoitering.

Within the room was a wide bed, an easy chair (soiled and rent), a low table made of processed wood, and an open wardrobe in which a skirt and a raccoon-tail collar hung from hooks. The room smelled mostly of Harriet's scent and slightly of must. An oddity—Rosen just noticed it—was the unframed Rouault, one of his clowns, scotchtaped to a wall.

"Whatchoo think, little rube?"

Rosen nodded his head. He was still breathing hard. He was no longer aroused. Harriet saw. She circled toward him and took his jowly head in her hands. Her hands were slim and warm.

"You lost it, huh, brother dwarf? Harriet get it back for you, and for your buddy too. You'll see. Right now I need the twenty-five big ones."

"Five fives?"

"Any way you got it, Bo."

Rosen removed his wallet. The noon sun sliced into the room and onto his hands which were chapped from the cold and trembled a little. Harriet took the bills, sat on the bed, crossed her legs, and counted the money, licking her fingers. To Rosen she didn't look right, she didn't seem to be in harmony with the cramped room. Her rich titian hair was closer in spirit to the wrinkled Rouault than to the grimy white walls. Her wide frontal bone tapered to a pointed, even demure, chin. Her skin was nice, but the false lashes that framed the brown clear eyes looked tawdry. Her heels were too high for the small room, her hips too broad, too mobile.

Now Rosen's legs were trembling. From the unaccustomed steep climb.

Harriet folded the bills and fitted them into her left shoe. Then looked up at him with shining eyes.

"Don't be afraid, lover. C'mon over to the bed and squat on my thighs."

"Squat?"

"Thas right."

Rosen did it.

"I like your piles," Harriet whispered.

"What?"

"Piles. You got a little extry back there. I could feel." She slithered her tongue into his ear: "Tell me bout this buddy of yours."

"Oh. I'd like to stop his hating."

August lunched at Dooley's Coffee Shop. It was one p.m., infested with lunchers. He watched Nick, the rangy short-order cook, adroitly cut and slice and flip and stretch and grin. Nick was a Greek, happy at his work, always grinning. August had no bone to pick with Nick. It wasn't Nick's fault that he was waiting as he always had to wait for a lousy sandwich. August didn't care for the other countermen, or for Lois the cashier. He unfurled his *Wall Street Journal* and the first name that seized his eye was Ham Jordan, the libidinous clown whom Carter brought with him from Georgia. By the time August's chicken salad sandwich was delivered the priapic Ham was squatting atop his head. And when August raised the sandwich to his mouth the pious buffoon interposed his jaws and bit first. Jordan had already died multiple deaths and now August would have to do him again. How though? Reflecting tensely, he sipped his coffee. Then he stood and went to the washroom. Someone was inside. A few minutes later the person emerged and August entered, lowering his head a little so as not to bludgeon the Hamclown. He had bludgeoned him before; this time he had in mind a Dantean terminus. The toilet stank, but that was even better. August locked the door behind him, went into the stall, raised the toilet seat and baptized the gross clown in the slimy undertow, keeping him immersed until he was indeed ready to meet his Jesus... When August returned to his small table it was occupied, his coffee and sandwich had been whisked away. The bussboy must have assumed he'd left. It was already 1:40.

The humpback was squatting on Harriet's thighs and fondling her breasts. They were nice breasts, though not large and only a little pendant. Small brown nipples. Harriet kissed his nose and set him down on the floor. Deftly, she undid his pants, pulled them down, and, lifting him onto her lap again, removed them. She fondled his piece.

Rosen gazed at her with soft eyes.

Meanwhile she had slipped a slim hand beneath his crotch and was gently tinkering with his stern. She smiled.

"This pile tissue, this little clit you got back there. I got just the thang. Does your buddy have this also?"

"What? Piles? I wouldn't know." Rosen, embarrassed, was no longer aroused.

"Feel mine," Harriet whispered.

"Yours?"

She unzipped her puce hotpants, took Rosen's hand and placed it on her stern.

"Feel with your finger, putzie."

He did. She had a tight, untroubled arsehole.

"Very nice," Rosen said. "Can I see?"

"Yes you can." She set Rosen on the bed and stood up in front of him with her back to him.

Slowly, with both hands, Rosen rolled Harriet's puce hotpants down to her thighs, and there it was: the lovely pink-white arse swelling like a bell from her waist to the fat rich globes. Rosen was aroused. But then he noticed her silhouette on the wall across from him and just about spit...

By 4:45, August had six gargoyle paperweights on his desk, six foul, lifeless heads, and his stomach hurt. His head throbbed about the temples and he was very angry. There was a lull. He stood up to go to the washroom, pausing at one of the secretary's desks in the outer office to read an item in a tabloid. A killer, huge and porcine, with a proclaimed admiration for the Nazis, and evidently a closet queer, had holed up in a factory building after gunning down six employees. His "last request" was for a plate of potato salad and a hot chocolate. This was duly honored. He finished the swinish repast, stuck the barrel of his shotgun in his throat and blew apart his head.

"How do you like that?" the secretary remarked to August. "Isn't that something?"

"It is, yes."

...She had a prick! Rosen couldn't believe it. Harriet saw he saw. She gave him a broad grin.

"What I say about the magic bone, little rube? This is it." She turned her front to him.

Rosen was standing, sweating heavily above his lip and on his forehead. "What... what are you?"

Harriet guffawed. "I'm the whole gig, baby. Those were real tits you squeezed. And this here's a real dick." She took hold of it, it was erect and long, though not especially thick. She had testicles too.

"You say this buddy of yours can't stop hating. You bend down now—what does he do?"

"Huh? August, you mean? Wall Street…"

"Ah. You bend down now, lover-guy."

Rosen watched her remove a tube of unguent from a drawer and smooth it onto her penis.

"This gonna feel real nice on your little clit and it gonna help your buddy with his hating, make him hate less, maybe stop altogether, though working where he does makes it a little harder. Ever take it up the dooley?"

"The what? No!"

Harriet laughed. "How much you willin to do to pull your buddy out of it?"

Like the person said, August stopped hating. Had to. Early in April he ordered his customary chicken salad sandwich at Dooley's Coffee Shop and choked on a small bone which should not have been in it.

The humpback Rosen, wearing his hair burned short in mourning, was among the half-dozen or so at August's funeral. Unexpectedly, one of the other mourners, a woman with carrot-red hair, approached him. She was somewhat beyond middle age and walked with rapid, nervous steps on high heels. She extended a slender calloused hand which she withdrew as soon as Rosen brushed it.

"You are?" she demanded.

"Rosen."

"Family?"

"In a sense."

These words made no impact. She said, "I was August's neighbor. What are you?"

"How do you mean?"

"Professionally."

"I am," Rosen said, "a blood donor."

She had already been gazing down at him in an askew kind of way. Rosen's words distorted her gaze even further. But before she had a chance to respond the dwarf pivoted on his tiny heel and shuffled—unsteadily—out of the wide, gloomy room, through a corridor, and into the street…

EAT YOUR GRIEF, CORA DANCE

EAT YOUR GRIEF, CORA DANCE

Osiris

killed in his own living room. Curled bleeding on his carpet. The police cut away the swatch of carpet where the body lay. As evidence. Months later his widow lives in the same three-room apartment, the gruesome rug cutout still in her living room. Her landlord insists he isn't responsible for replacing the carpet.

Osiris the listless one

killed man was disabled, black. His widow is "low-rent" housing development, Flushing, NY

According to Plutarch, "Osiris' body was washed up upon the Syrian shore at Byblos. The chest containing the body was cast up into a tree which grew around it. Isis obtained possession of the tree."

black. City agencies exist, are charged to redress these grievances. Their phone numbers are in the directory under "City..."

Unable to revive Osiris wholly, Isis contrived to revive him sufficiently to conceive a son by him. Horus.

widow's name is Dance. She says: My Floyd fought in two wars for this country. Our baby died in stillbirth while he was fighting in Korea. Now...this.

Another version has Horus emerging whole out of his mother's

*menstrual discharge. Are we referring here to Horus or to the goddess
Hathor? Osiris is, in any case, the key. Osiris*

if you can't locate them under "City," try "State," though I am certain
they are under "City." What is it you want, Mrs.... Dance?

*Is the sufferer with all life, but at the same time he is the source of
revival. He is plant growth and animal growth. Dead, he is yet the
growing motive for all living things. He may be seen then as our first
anarchist.*

yes, the carpeting. Money as well? That's liable to be complicated.
Your husband was gainfully employed? He was disabled. The carpeting is frankly between you and your landlord. The money

*Chomsky cites Rudolph Rocker's definition of anarchism as opposing
not only the "exploitation of man" but the "dominion of man over
man." As for distinguishing anarchism from "socialism," the true
anarchist steadfastly refuses to render to the state what is properly the
individual's. In this respect anarchism might be regarded (in
Chomsky's words) as the "libertarian wing of socialism."*

killed in his own living room. His bad leg dangling, the rest of him
curled like a child, bleeding. His hip pocket and wallet severed from
his trousers with the same knife that stabbed him multiple times (sev-
enteen, according to the police report). A police technician cut away
the swatch of bloody carpeting for further analysis. Cora

*If Osiris is our first anarchist, surely Horus must be our first royalist.
Lifting up out of the menstrual waste he straddles his birth. From the
vast reaches of heaven, in the realm of pure fire, he is the God-falcon
who yet draws sustenance from the low: in mountain and desert, in
primordial slime. Horus/Osiris. Systole, diastole.*

Dance thumbs through the telephone directory. She walks to the
supermarket. Observe the dislocated gait. Childless greyhaired black
widow-lady. Her husband's insurance policy contained no provision
for "crime-related demise."

*O functionary, yours is a pauper spirit. You are white and your calling
is to pronounce on the fate of Cora Dance. Is this not how you would
put it? Consider: function in accord with station. The gracile atten-*

dant sets the pink princely child on the water lily. If the lily were vertebrate it would experience an exquisite gravity. This figure is obviously drawn from royalty, and yet we refer to an essential hierarchy; indeed the metaphor is adapted (loosely) from the "Egyptian Book of the Dead." There are cognate passages in the Buddhist "Dhammapada," in Aristotle's "Ethics"...

small fucking consolation.

...We haven't quite framed the thought. Bakunin was a promethean figure, was he not? Initially. Bakunin's anarchism was a "No! in thunder!" to exploitation, to structure imposed from the top, to any delimitation of individual rights. A Melvillian presence. And like Melville he ended finally by compromising not with the "system," but in accord with the Tao, with the nature of systems. There being no other "way" (double meaning intended). Are we thinking here of Bakunin or Kropotkin? Or of the German Stirner? Never mind, the principle holds.

the police have a suspect, black kid from the neighborhood. Name of Ditts. Didn't admit it. Not yet. Motive? We're working on that. Dope money probably. Boogie money.

Our stance is clinical, phenomenological. What else can it reasonably be? Observe that dead catbird on the lawn. Watch now how the dahlias bloom. Woman is fundament. Eat your grief, Cora Dance. As for

as it turned out Ditts had an air-tight alibi. Was shooting up in some tenement basement. Fresh tracks and some other junkie confirm. Lock their ass up for breaking and entering. No right being on that property, not theirs.

Consolation, Blofeld in his recent study of Taoism refers to " 'dragon veins,' invisible lines running down from the sky into the mountains and along the earth, whose function is rather similar to that of psychic channels within the body, as in Yoga..." These "dragon veins" are faith. Faith in what is (faith in "what seems" is something else, truly), in spite of personal grief. Those who possess this faith —and blacks are not excluded—will find their dope, so to speak, in Jesus, Buddha, Zoroaster, whatever.

a neighbor managed to get hold of one of Cora Dance's relatives in Tupelo, Mississippi, and yesterday a grand niece bussed up to New York and will be staying with Widow Dance so that she won't be alone. This same neighbor is trying to raise money on the block to replace Cora Dance's living room carpet. Since the landlord refuses to budge on this.

A homely instance, an emblem: We read the other day of a young nursing mother from Wales who attempted to suckle a baby bat (Eumops perotis), starving for want of insects this cold summer. Of course the creature died; though not before infecting the young mother, so that she could no longer suckle her true child. This was Wales, U.K., of the planet Earth, you understand, and not Cockayne or Erewhon. Cora's got to take her

turning the pages of the telephone directory with unsteady fingers, Cora Dance unexpectedly recalls something from her youth in Tupelo, Mississippi—a Choctaw Indian family: father, wife, two children, all in tatters, gazing in through a store window at a floor-model radio for sale, gazing with their faces up against the glass, with an expression that...she couldn't then describe. Somehow she feels she understands it now, this expression. Understands now forty-odd years later north of

Lumps. Like the rest of us.

Mississippi.

MURDER ON LORD NORTH STREET

MURDER ON LORD NORTH STREET

The murder of L occurred on a Tuesday, midday, the sun in Capricorn. (Intractable memory...) Bent was in a lavatory on Lord North Street.

Bent is a lifelister. Birds. He's spotted and identified 188 species. This is not an impressive number to the accomplished birder, but then Bent has seen specific individuals of a given species numerous times. A favorite loon, a particular soiled robin, a boat-tailed grackle with her implausible yellow eyes.

Lionel Bent is on the tube, the District Line, he has just passed Hammersmith, he is standing, smoking a Players ("navy cut"), he is off to Kew...

Lila is reading Bataille; she recently read a volume of Lawrence's stories. Blood pushing, blood pulling: this engages her. She is sitting on a wooden bench next to an elderly woman in a small grove of hairy birches (*Betula pubescens*) opposite a rill.

Around the time of L's murder Bent removed himself, with decidedly mixed feelings, out of his eyrie in Notting Hill to...Flushing.

Bent grinds his cigarette with his boot-sole, Lila turns the page. Just south of Turnham Green Bent glimpses something through the window out of the corner of his left eye—a rudely-fashioned wooden cross anchored in a sward. Poorly anchored in fact, as if planted by a child to mark the passing of a bird. (Cain's jawbone. Unremitting memory.)

Bent has had his pee and, ascending the steep lavatory stair, bumps into a thin man in a bowler. The man has a pallor, the planes of his face are not right. Yet there is a subtle address and delicate irony in the slight bow, in the tone in which he says, "Frightfully sorry." Bent catches the luminous red eyes only fleetingly, replies, "Not a'tall. No harm done." Lord North Street.

Lila is wearing jodhpurs. She is a rapid reader, even of Bataille. Bataille watches himself watch himself vomit. "Lovely day," Lila says. The elderly woman turns to her, smiles, her customary reserve mitigated by the sun and birches, by the loon in the rill. "Yes, 'tis. Lovely."

Flushing is across the ocean, in New York in fact, in a borough called Queens. Leo, an old acquaintance, phoned to report a position opening: an associate professorship in Bent's "field" at a certain college in Flushing. There would be three or four other applicants, was Bent "seriously interested?"

As Bent was trundling past Turnham Green on the District Line, Lila was negotiating an exceedingly French piece of pornography in Bataille: the protagonist, who has had himself trussed to a wooden cross, is being fellated by a pubescent girl in an eagle headdress. Lila is in Kew, sitting on a bench in a grove of birches, fronting a rill. Lionel Bent has sat down next to her. He is wearing a brown hound's-tooth tweed hacking-jacket, loose-fitting cords, a blue woolen sweater, and thick-soled sandals. The jacket he picked up for eight pounds in a second-hand shop on Portobello Road. On his head he is sporting a bowler. Lila laughs.

Bent assured Leo (nervous Leo) that he was "seriously interested"; asked Leo to forward whatever data he had on the bloke who would be doing the hiring.

The elderly woman with the dignified mien says to Lila: "Lovely day." Lila, absorbed in Bataille's crucifixion, raises her head: "Yes, 'tis. Lovely." "And such lovely trees." "Yes." Just then a loon surfaces in the rill and yodels. The elderly woman smiles: "Now there's a clever fellow." Leo has sent Bent a small dossier on Lewisohn, the department chairman, and Bent has already read one of Lewisohn's three volumes in the British Museum. Then, after taking care of some "business" on Lord North Street, he has caught his tube at Westminster. Off to Kew...

"Flushing?" Lila laughs. "But what can that be? And where did you get that bowler. It looks quite, quite silly." "There's my loon," Lionel Bent says. "You see, he greets us. What is that you're reading?" He reads a bit over Lila's shoulder. "Buggery on a cross, is it? Flushing, to answer your question, is a hamlet in the borough of Queens. Which is to say, New York." "Yes," Lila says. "And you've bloodied your hand."

The elderly woman has breeding. And something more: a subtle manner of expression, with a delicate, even iridescent, irony as one of its components. Or so it seems to Lila, moist now beneath her jodhpurs, observing Bataille observe his protagonist appraise himself on the wooden cross, the eagle-child on her knees, her small hands clasping the soles of his bleeding feet, petal mouth at the distended prick.

Lionel Bent has read all three of Professor Lewisohn's undistinguished volumes. He has sent Leo the details regarding his arrival in Flushing. The memory of the child's cross near Turnham Green preoccupies Bent as he finishes his pee and, mounting the fetid stair, bangs flush into a bony man in a bowler, jarring the hat from his head. Recovering, Bent glares at the fellow, who returns the hard look with his red eyes. Suddenly they are scuffling.

Among the books Bent has selected to take with him to Flushing are a guide to North American birds, some Henry Vaughan, a slender volume of his own verse, and Lila's Bataille.

Lila: "Shall we look at trees?" Bent nods, Lila takes his hand. "How did you bloody your hand?" Bent smiles: "I killed a chap. This was his bowler. It is, as you said, a poor fit. *Quercus ilex:* what a handsome holm oak." "Oak?" Lila says. "It looks awfully like holly." "I think I'm going to like your Bataille," Bent says. "No doubt," Lila says. "But will they let you into Flushing with it?"

"In case you're wondering, it pays well. For an academy position, that is." Leo is expatiating as he drives Bent from the New York airport to Flushing. "But I should tell you that the people you are up against are not slouches. Particularly two of the four. The problem is that you haven't published anything for what, five years? But if you can get beyond the committee interview, then you will have your chance to impress Lewisohn. What in hell have you been doing in England all this time?" "Not much," Bent says.

When Bent emerges from the lavatory on Lord North Street it is raining, but when he arrives at Kew nearly two hours later, the rain has stopped, the sun has partially penetrated the mist, people are quietly enjoying the gardens, Kew is as vivid (nearly) as Seurat. Lionel and Lila have collected spruce cones. When they embrace Bent interposes a cone between their hips. Lila smiles: "Bataille." "You see," Lionel says. "I know him without having read him."

Bent has bussed from Flushing to a beach called Jones, on the Atlantic. A cool, rainy day, nobody out. A least tern, a common tern, an osprey wheeling high above the surf. Bent is moving deliberately from west to east. Ten or fifteen meters ahead he sees something stuck in the sand: a cross. Two driftwood sticks of unequal size with a quahog shell in the center, delicately fastened with seaweed. The cross is about a foot and a half high and is anchored in the sand at an angle tilting toward the sea.

What to deploy against memory? Considering patiently and not so patiently this question is (to respond silently to Leo) what Bent has been "doing" for the last several years. Lao-tse, Li Po, Bergson, Bachelard are among those who have addressed themselves to that vital, waxen blossom, whose roots are mineral, circean…Memory. Lionel Bent means to break new ground. Hence L: *murdered*.

The pale bony personage with his unsurpassable bearing holds his bowler in his hand while he pisses. He resembles the figure of death in Resnais' *Last Year at Marienbad*. Bent, swiftly descending the stair, crashes into him as he is replacing the bowler on his head. The hat trips down the stair and rolls beneath a urinal. Fierce stares inflicted at close range, but mannerly words, and even, absurdly, handshakes. "So sorry." "Not a'tall." "There goes your hat." "No harm done."

Bent: "Tell me about Lewisohn." Leo: "You read some of his stuff?" Bent: "Yes." Leo: "Well, what do you want to know?" Bent: "Everything."

Bussing from Jones Beach to a cramped tattoo parlor in south Flushing, Bent spots an eastern phoebe on a telephone wire. A charming disjunct image with its Giacometti wedge-head. The sensitive rude cross perhaps marked the burial of a phoebe, or, more likely, a waterbird. If it is not possible to blunt it, why not become it, that cicatrix: memory.

Once encouraged to talk, the elderly woman is unexpectedly voluble. "Did you read about the murder? In the *Evening Standard?* This chap had two y's in his genies. I never heard of that before. Have you? He killed a girl, you know. Throttled her right here. In Kew. Behind the sitka spruces, I think it was. The police caught up with him straightaway, stuck him right in gaol."

"Tell me about *The Petrified Forest.*" Bent: "Ah, Leslie Howard on the American frontier. He nullified his past." Lila: "How did he do that?" Bent: "By selecting his own death." Lila: "And Bette Davis?" Bent: "Young Bette Davis was, oddly, sweet memory..." The cross in the sand travelled with Lionel Bent to the tattoo parlor; he contemplated it while the technician (robed in his own tattoos) etched the letters: L I L A on Bent's left wrist where previously he had worn his watch.

The interview was two-fold: first the screening with a committee of six. Then (assuming the committee didn't void him) alone with Lewisohn. Ass-back, camel-back, Volkswagen-Rabbit-back...Bent picked up the rather obvious frequencies and changed mounts deftly. For the committee. It was only when he got to Lewisohn that he subtly displayed his tattoo and witnessed Lewisohn's response veer from "surprised disapproval," to "modest curiosity," to "disapproval" again, but with its liberal Jewish correlate: "guilt," to (this would happen afterwards, offstage) "final—ambivalent—approval."

"Become memory"? Void its limitless capacity to distill attar from greyness, from grief, only to set this scented pastel lie on casters and send it scampering down-mountain away from you. How then?

When the imperial personage in the bowler raised his bony left arm as if in defense, Bent detected a cursive design, or charm, etched into his wrist. Afterwards Bent saw that it was in fact a single word: PAST. It was this word that a nonplussed Lewisohn read on applicant

Bent's wrist. Bent returned to London on Thursday. The following Tuesday Lewisohn notified him that he had gotten the position. After a commemorative breakfast on Wednesday, Bent sent Lewisohn this telegram: HAVE DECIDED TO TURN OFFER DOWN.

The sea air is fragrant. Bent at the ocean smells the refracted scent of spruce. The decomposed head of a waterbird lies on the hard sand at the foot of the cross.

After the interviews Bent returned to his bed-sitting room in Flushing, removed his tie, put on rough shoes and an ulster, and bussed to Jones Beach. Not cold, but misty, nobody out. Bent had returned to England with the favorable news. He was to meet Lila at Kew. But between the time he went into the lavatory on Lord North Street, had his encounter with the bony man in the bowler, and emerged again outside, the weather had abruptly worsened. Nonetheless Bent entered the underground at St. James, got on his District Line, lit a Players, and closed his eyes. By the time he reached the terminus the rain had stopped, though the air was still quite damp. Lila was waiting at the trysting spot, sitting on her *Evening Standard* which was spread on a bench near their spruce grove.

Bent is supine in Notting Hill. He would seem to be contemplating Flushing. His arms (crossed at the wrists) lie on his chest.

Create first the possibilities for a "secure" future; then—with a stroke—obliterate it. While jackal-memory plunders the "what ifs," apply this finale: zero your current.

Lila is waiting for Lionel in a deserted thicket facing their rill. She is standing, holding a sheet of newspaper atop her head against the rain. Something about the way her body is planted is not right. When Lionel Bent comes closer he sees she is pointing to the grass near the water. A cross: two uneven-sized twigs with a spruce cone at its juncture and tied together with vine, is stuck into the ground; and next to it a loon (*Gavia immer*), dead and...headless; the head wholly excised from the body, nowhere in sight.

PLATTSBURGH

PLATTSBURGH

Leap Year: fool

March 1:   Cora D. reported dead. A suicide. The heat in her house is turned off, her radio is turned off, her basset hound is almost impounded, her house is locked and boarded-up, this last a "standard procedure to preclude the possibility of burglary" (Lieutenant V. of the Plattsburgh City Police).

Feb. 28:   Cora D. was on her way to work in the Young Adult's Division of the Plattsburgh Public Library (University Branch), driving east on Highway 24, when she saw something bunched and brown on the road ahead. To herself she said, "owl." Then aloud she said, "My God, it's an owl." She pulled her car onto the shoulder and knelt to the bird, which after a moment she recognized as a great horned owl. Its eyes were closed, but Cora could see the rhythmic pulsing of its breast. She gathered the owl in her arms with the intention of taking it to her vet whose office was ten miles or so east of the library.

Leap Year: an enemy of boundaries fool wears multiple masks makes no distinctions between associations and meanings between usual days and leap year days

March 1:   Officer Cora S. (another Cora) received the call at 8 p.m. on Feb. 29. A female who did not leave her name said simply, soberly—as Officer S. recalls—that Cora D. was dead, a suicide. "I thought you would want to know," the caller said.

Feb. 28:   What happened next was astonishing: the owl suddenly extended its talons, dug into Cora D.'s chest, flapped its wings twice as

47

if to secure its "perch," then fell back into shock. When Cora tried to extract one now bloody talon from her chest where it had penetrated the skin through her woolen sweater, the creature lifted its wings just a bit and sunk its talons deeper into her flesh.

Leap Year: fool lays the host out on a wide strip of basswood and proceeds to take apart the flesh body he unjoints the joints the bones which he separates from the skeleton he wipes with a catalpa leaf catalpa is rife in Plattsburgh fool has already ravished the flesh

March 1: Officers Moffo and Svobodzinski (called "Ski") were driving their radio car in the area of the university campus when they received the call. They proceeded to the late Cora D.'s house to close it up. When they arrived the door was unlocked, the heat was on, the radio was playing "an opera or something," Moffo recalled. A light had been left on in the bathroom, and the basset hound was reclining on a scatter rug in front of the sofa.

Feb. 28: Cora D.'s Honda Civic was still running. She didn't get back into her car. It must have been cold outside—she could see the vapor rising from her mouth and nose. Not though from the owl's beak; the bird lay perfectly still against her breast except for its breathing, soft, rhythmic, human-sounding. Unless it was her own heart. She wasn't certain. She was not at all cold. She felt strangely calm standing near her car on the road's shoulder with the great horned owl locked into her breast. Its distinctive "horns" or ear tufts were pulled back against its head. It occurred to Cora that aside from bird guides and magazines, she had only once in her life seen an owl, a screech owl in a catalpa tree when she had been a child in Wilkes-Barre.

Leap Year: with the refined bones a new old flesh is supplied fool works dexterously unconsciously it is after all Plattsburgh stinks of flesh smirking he strips naked and spreads himself out on the highway owls and hawks and carrion birds circle

March 1: Moffo patted the basset hound who gazed at him through one bemused, heavy-lidded eye. The name-tag on the hound's collar said "Caruso." Moffo said to his partner: "How do you like that? The dog's name is Caruso." "What's that?" "Caruso? He was an opera singer." Just then the doorbell sounded and someone came in. It was Pat the carpenter. "This is the one gotta be boarded-up, right?"

"Right, Pat. Who sent you?" "The Lieutenant."

Feb. 28: So far nobody had really noticed her. But now people were glancing at her from their cars as they sped by. A good many cars passed before one stopped, a pickup with two men in it. "Anything wrong, lady?" Then the other man said, "What's she got on her chest?" Cora D., unmoving, with the owl motionless (except for its breathing) at her breast, smiled. That's what one of the men told the police afterwards. "She smiled. I couldn't make it out. I thought she had some kind of baby in her arms. Like a—a mongoloid or something." His buddy was nodding his head. "Yeah, that's just what it looked like—some kind of baby."

While the two men were staring at Cora D. another car stopped, and then another. A woman in one of the stopped cars took hold of her husband's wrist: "Gerry, it's an owl—she's holding an owl!" She got out of her car and went up to Cora. "Is it hurt?" "It's stuck," Cora said. "Its talons are stuck in my chest." By now other people had gathered round. A man with an imperative manner said, "It's going to have to be killed. No way its claws will relax unless its killed." Cora shook her head decisively: "I don't want that. I don't want killing."

Leap Year: an owl silently landed next to the recumbent naked fool and looking for a route through the toughened skin commenced to tear at fool's rectum fool distended his rectum so that the owl not only hacked with its beak but eventually succeeded in wedging its entire head into the stinking hole whereupon fool snapped close his rectum imprisoning the owl's head

March 1: Pat the carpenter said, "Where's the body?" Moffo shrugged: "Haven't a clue. Gimme a cigarette." The carpenter shook out a Camel. He said, "I'm thirsty." "Check out the fridge," Ski said. Pat went into the kitchen: "Orange juice, prune juice and milk," he called out. "No beer, guys. Also club soda. It looks flat." Moffo shouted back: "Pour Ski some prune juice. I'll take orange." Ski laughed: "No prune. Orange for me too. Right from the container, Pat. Don't touch no glasses." "Why no glasses?" Moffo wanted to know. "In case it's a homicide, Mof. I mean it could be a homicide, right?"

Feb. 28: A Mercury Monarch stopped and a woman stepped out. "I am a registered nurse," she announced as she approached Cora D. "May I?" she said, taking hold of one of the owl's legs above its talons. But immediately the owl raised its wings and sank its talons a notch deeper into Cora's flesh. It seemed to do this instinctively, not even opening its eyes. Cora winced but made no sound. The nurse said: "This Honda is yours, right? I'll drive it and you to University Hospital. My husband will follow in our car. We'd better get started."

Leap year: fool has a cap fool has a tail getting up off the highway he laughs his high-pitched laugh as the owl furiously struggles flapping its wings swiping with its talons fool wiggles to a public phone

March 1: "Good juice," Moffo said, handing the container to Ski. "What happens to the dog?" "The pound," Ski said. "It's a shame," Moffo said. "Nice dog." "They only kill them if no one wants them," Ski explained. "Maybe this guy—what's his name?" "Caruso." "Maybe someone'll adopt him—Caruso. Hey, I just thought of something. If it's a homicide how come we're boarding up the place?" "No homicide," Pat said. "Suicide. That's what the Lieutenant said."

Feb. 28: In the emergency room of Plattsburgh University Hospital the resident physician had prematurely greying hair. He appraised Cora D.'s situation and said: "It would be a lot easier for you if we destroy the bird. It may be easier for the bird as well—it might be seriously hurt." "I don't think so," Cora said. "I don't think it's seriously hurt. Please don't talk about killing it." The physician shrugged. "I'd better give you a tranquilizer, Mrs. D."

Leap Year: sometimes called the spirit of disorder fool transports his penis wrapped round and round like a garden hose in a box and his vulva on his head when he speaks into the telephone receiver his voice is female evidently it's droll to be female in Plattsburgh

March 1: The basset hound started making like Caruso only when Moffo tried to coax him into the radio car. Nearby neighbors were alerted, and one, a man leading a dog—*another* basset hound— rapidly approached the officers. "What are you doing to Caruso?" he demanded angrily. From within the car Officer Svobodzinski demanded in turn: "Who the hell are you?" "I'm Mrs. D.'s neighbor and friend." "Your friend is dead," Ski said curtly. "What? You're crazy. She and my wife are right now visiting an acquaintance in the hospital. University Hospital." This declaration was received in silence. Moffo and Ski exchanged a look. It had begun to snow.

Feb. 28: While the physician carefully worked the owl's talons with a pair of forceps, a nurse wearing protective mittens restrained the owl. Cora did not look at the young physician who reminded her powerfully of someone (or perhaps of a circumstance) she could not place. After a time the owl's talons responded to the delicate pinching and pulling of the forceps by spreading, loosening. At last the talons on both feet were extracted from Cora D.'s flesh. The nurse carried the owl outside with the intention of transferring it to another room until a decision was made about what to do with it. But as soon as she got outside the creature stirred, opened his eyes, unfurled his wings. The nurse panicked and let go of the owl—who lifted, hovering for a moment on outspread wings, then flew silently out of sight into the frigid Plattsburgh night...

Leap Year: it is 7:55 p.m. fool reports Cora D.'s suicide while scratching his back against a corner of the booth then outside breaks wind thus ejecting the owl who after a befogged moment scampers then flies into the Plattsburgh night meanwhile his stupendous fart has released the snows fool is hungry he rifles Cora D.'s fridge turns on her radio ignores her hound uses her toilet

March 1: Officer Moffo handed the leash which held the immovable and now snowed-upon Caruso to his partner, then accompanied Cora D.'s neighbor into his house. The man, who identified himself as Mr. Moffet, phoned the patient's room at University Hospital, speaking first with his wife and then with Cora D. He handed the phone to Moffo who said: "Mrs. D.? There's been a strange—uh, mixup, Mrs. D. I think you'd better come home right away..."

Feb. 28: Denise Moffet, Cora D.'s friend, was notified by a nurse and it was she who drove the sutured Cora home after the procedure in the University Hospital emergency room.

Leap Year: ◯

"ENTROPOLOGY"

"ENTROPOLOGY"

G: "Old Carney the lifer with the shot lungs. What he spits up after chow is how I feel about my life. Since you want to know."

D: "I did everything they wanted, but when I went before the parole board they denied me. Okay, next time I'm up is in sixteen months, and when I come this time I'm ready with newspaper items and letters and affidavits on my case. Have it all real neat in a folder. But they take the folder from me at the door so that I can't quote any of the stuff that has a bearing on my case. Then they deny me."

G has been in Point Hope State Prison since last Christmas, twice sentenced to die by firing squad. Twice his execution was stayed. The issue: capital punishment. Among G's unwanted allies is the ACLU, who after G said, "I killed two humans, didn't I? I deserve to get killed, I don't want your pity," wired: "REGRETS. REFUSE TO PERMIT YOU TO TURN US INTO MURDERERS."

D doesn't stop accumulating material on his case. When he comes before the board sixteen months later he has memorized about eighty pages of data: newspaper items, testimonial letters, character references, affidavits. His entire hearing takes less than fifteen minutes. He is denied a third time.

G is news. It's winter but past Christmas, nearly Lent. Point Hope State Prison, south of Salt Lake City, comprises several buildings, among them a vacated slaughterhouse. The meathooks in the ceiling are gone. Small nodes where the hooks were, though plastered over, are still visible. The large freezer has been transformed into eight solitary confinement cells. G occupies two of these cells. Previously he had occupied one, but a few months ago the thick wall between the cells was razed to accomodate the Press, the Media. G has been fasting.

"How come you're not eating?" a reporter wants to know.

G does not respond.

She had been told it was "stomach problems"—only to learn (fourteen years after the surgery) that her Fallopian tubes had been removed. She is D's stepmother. When she found out what had been done she said: "Wiley and me wanted children desperate—we was crazy about them." Wiley, her husband, long dead. She still lives on the reservation.

D: "Yeah, she's alive. Still on the reservation. We write. She sees me too sometimes, though it's real expensive for her to come all the way from Tulsa. Soon's I get out I'm going to spend a good long time with her too."

G's been in institutions of one kind or another off and on his whole life. He's thirty-five now. When he was ten and living with foster parents in southern Idaho his grade school teacher asked her students to draw self-portraits. G drew a beat-up old shoe.

It's nearly Lent and G is news. The news is delivered by NEX-XON: "For those who draw inspiration from America's history of pioneer courage, the country between Salt Lake City and what is whimsically referred to as the Point Hope Meat Factory, thirty miles to the south along the flank of the Utah valley, is a panorama of the old wild west. For much of this distance the thruway is a scribble of neon billboards, fast food outlets and light industry. But as the alkali beds become hills and the hills mountains, nearly every other house seems to have a goat or a cow or a horse or two grazing in the front yard..."

D is in a state prison in Louisiana. Been spending all his off-hours in the prison library reading about the law. Has developed open sores on his lower back and buttocks from nervously grinding his hips against the hard chair. Now he stands or squats while reading. He's already filed suit against the Louisiana Board of Corrections for denying his rights. Got several other ideas in his head too. To the other inmates D is a "writ writer," that is a con who files suits.

G's executioners had already been enlisted when this flap happened. This capital punishment thing. Five male citizens from Point Hope township (the union statute defines a state prison executioner as a "para-institution employee," which means he must reside in the prison county), each firing an army M-16, one of them firing blanks. One of them has a bum cartridge in his breech but none of them knows which one.

Other inmates consult D because of his knowledge of the law. But he doesn't have any buddies. He's so caught up with accumulating stuff on his case that you can't really talk with him. Besides he's a Comanche Indian. Or part Comanche anyway. Forty years old, he's in only his second stretch in the joint. The word is he's "light."

G says, "Even as a kid I used to look at grown people in such a way as to make them uneasy. I don't know why. None of the other kids had that effect on them. Just me." G says this to himself. To the media people, literary agents, publicity hounds, he says almost nothing. He has drunk only water for three days.

NEXXON nationwide: "Listen, my fellow Americans, to what passes for logic among the radical lawyer coterie who are G's self-anointed defenders. I am quoting now: 'The need for a stay of execution is imperative for several reasons, notwithstanding the prisoner's assertion that he wishes to be executed. First, there may have been juridical errors in the original trial; second, Prisoner may have waived his constitutional rights without fully understanding them. Finally, Utah's capital punishment statute may be unconstitutional.'

"Observe, if you will, how many 'mays' there are in this thing. These so-called civil libertarians do not even pretend to be certain of what they are doing, yet they are evidently more than ready to short-change the taxpayers of this great state, as well as inconvenience the entire country, in the process of exploring their uncertainties."

The five Point Hope citizens have their M-16's. The rifles have been checked out to them, but not the ammo. One of them got hold of some ammo and killed a buck deer. Shot it to hell too.

G: "If I feel like killing, it don't really matter who gets it. Killing's like puking. If your shit got to belly up don't matter at all who is left with your stink—as long as you puke it the fuck out."

D says, "I'm not light. I'm no different than anyone else. Only I can't be like anyone else because I'm stuck in here. I did my time. I deserve to get out. I'll tell you what: they don't parole me this time I'm gonna sue the balls offa them. I know how to do it too."

The executioners play cards together, poker. They're awfully itchy. They're sort of in the middle of something, all this about G on the TV and in the papers, and they ain't getting any richer either. Though everyone else seems to. You should see the cameras and slick operators and hoopla in and around Point Hope. The five executioners play cards together at Two's house. It's mid-afternoon. One, Two, Three and Five are there. Four comes late, says, "The sun is real hot outside and I seen this beggar laying in the shadow. In the little bit of shade near the building. Any of you see him?"

A prison psychologist found G to be a "classic sociopath," dead to feeling, or any concern beyond his own immediate gratification. And Warden Boyd Earle pronounced him a "sick mutt." Several times in the past G tried to take his own life, most recently slashing his wrists with a broken light bulb. Now the ACLU insists that he be force-fed lest his fast (five days tomorrow) kill him. However, sources close to the case remain skeptical. As much as he claims he wants to die, lots of folks don't believe him, are sure he's running some kind of scam to attract attention and actually stay alive. Besides, G knows that suicides can't be donors. And he wants to donate his organs.

Here's something: D got slashed, stabbed and beat up real bad. Yesterday after evening chow outside the library. They didn't find out who did it yet, but the speculation is it's mixed up with him being a faggot.

G's family has already discussed the division of G's worldly goods, including parts of his body. One of his cousin Elaine's children hopes to get his pineal gland. "I wish I could get G's brain," his aunt Sheryl said with a smile. "I always wanted to go to college."

D hemorrhaged last night and was rushed to Gulf Shore General Hospital. This morning the *Orleans Sun-Ledger* came out with some strange information. Their ace police reporter, who has unimpeachable underworld contacts throughout the South and the Southwest, wrote that what happened to D had nothing to do with his alleged homosexuality. Another con, YY, who was serving four consecutive life sentences for property theft and murder, told Ace's source that Warden Major Ledbetter had supplied YY with a knife and the instructions to "make sure D don't go to the library any more." YY said, "I cut D on both sides of his neck and arms, and I sliced three fingers off his right hand to make it hard for him to turn book pages. When I gave him back the knife Warden Major gave me a real wide grin and said he'd see what he could do for me."

Executioner Four: "I seen this beggar—I guess that's what he was—laying outside. The sun was high and real hot, but he was in this small blotch of shadow the building made. He was laying there and licking his fingers—like a dog or a cat would do. Any of you see him?"

NEXXON: "It evidently meant little to the killer who inherited his bodily organs. Indeed he even took to fasting in the last week or so. Denying himself food so that his appearance became even more extreme than it had been. When a reporter from this network asked him what he was trying to prove, G mentioned the name of Mahatma Gandhi, the Hindu politician of a few decades ago, whom the great Winston Churchill once described as a 'naked little fakir.' With one important difference however: Gandhi didn't have anything but curried rice to eat, while G denied himself what according to Warden Boyd Earle and to Point Hope Prison inmates is the best and most varied institutional food west of Indiana."

G's executioners are irritated with all the waiting around. They exchange gibes about which one of them's going to get the bum cartridge. Then One, Two, Three and Five ask Four to explain about that beggar of his, and Four repeats what he said before. The others egg him on for a while before losing interest.

When the NAACP joins the ACLU in opposing G's execution, G says: "You ain't got nothing to do with me dead or alive, Sambos. Butt out!"

Meanwhile the American people appear to be wearying of the G spectacle. At least that's what the polls say. This morning the state's highest court refuses a third stay of execution and sentences the prisoner to die.

A bandaged, partially fingerless D is returned to his prison cell in Louisiana.

(NEXXON's people have flushed megabucks into this G business, and now their harried researchers have come up with a sidelight item designed to recharge dwindling viewer interest—until the final boom.)

NEXXON: "Amazing as it seems, in these his last days, G, the admitted murderer of two innocent citizens, has been carrying on an intense correspondence with a ten year old girl from Casper, Wyoming, and has given her more than $1500 in gifts.

"G has written her fourteen letters from his cell at the Point Hope facility. The first letter was sent last May 2, in response to a note from April Kemp, who wrote to the condemned killer because, in her words, 'I thought he might be lonesome.'

"April, the daughter of Mr. and Mrs. Stew Kemp, is a kind of local celebrity herself—which evidently made G feel closer to her—as the only female second baseman in the Casper Little League. Known as 'Jud,' the sixty pound tomboy fourth grader gets straight A's and says that poetry is her favorite subject. After baseball, that is.

"Through his uncle, T.D. Remy (who also acts as his agent), G purchased a complete 8-millimeter movie outfit for the Kemps. Stew Kemp films his daughter's games and then they study the films to 'improve her technique.' Her 'technique' must be a darn good one, because April batted third in the lineup and led her team in base hits, while making just three errors at second base in twenty Little League games this past season.

"As the relationship with her 'pen pal' continued, April worked even harder at her baseball skills so that she would 'do real good for G.' G's letters, meanwhile, became more openly affectionate, full of expressions like, 'Sweet girl,' and 'Love,' and 'Baby.'

"Childish questions like, 'What's your favorite animal?' were answered with philosophic lines from the poet Wilhelm Blake: 'Tiger, Tiger, burning bright...' with the added comment: 'kinda nice, huh?' G explained that the tiger was powerful, beautiful and fearless, and was his favorite animal.

"He constantly expressed a desire to either talk on the phone with April or have her visit him, but the prison authorities never granted either request.

"Explaining his solitary confinement to the young girl, G wrote, 'I always had a hard time with rules. Some rules just didn't make any sense to me.' And about his life in general, G said he 'messed this one up real bad' and wanted to end it, but hoped he might have another opportunity in 'the next life.'

"The Kemps are admittedly hard-up and thrive on the publicity. Stew Kemp is a custodian at his daughter's school and is currently dabbling in Real Estate to increase his income. 'I think April will be up there in the Most Valuable Player category this season,' Stew boasted, adding, 'Until G started helping us out we were just too poor to give April the things she needed for her career. It's kinda weird, to tell you the truth. April wrote to G to comfort him and here he is making us happy.'

"As a parting gift, G sent April a picture book entitled 'Jackie Robinson: Second Baseman,' with a brief letter that ended with the words: 'Farewell, Love. Hit one into the gap for me.' "

D gone. According to Ace's source inside the prison, three nights ago, late, "D barricaded his cell bars with his mattress and blankets, then squatting in the middle of his cell he lit a match to his nearly forty pounds of newspaper articles, testimonial letters, character references, affidavits...No way the guards could get to him in time."

Death week, dawn. Prisoner led into the cramped makeshift courtroom adjoining the kill-yard. His scarred wrists are manacled. He is wearing faded grey prison livery, is gaunt from fasting, with an intense yet vacant look about his eyes. Asked by the judge whether he has anything to say, G, head bowed, whispers: "I hear I'm to be seated. And masked. I don't want that. I want to stand with my eyes open." Explaining that he is not empowered to alter the details of the execution, the judge does not honor this request. Which leaves only the time to be set. "I am going to set it at 7:30 a.m., Thursday," the judge says, "in accordance with a request from the Media. Do you request another time? You must understand, however, that if you do the chances are it will be turned down." "I don't request anything," G replies.

The executioners furnished with ammo, one cartridge each, Warden Boyd Earle alone knows which is the blank. They do it, perform smartly for NEXXON and the cameras, for the American public, who after wearying of all the shilly-shallying have expressed a renewed interest in the thing, in G's death jig (which is over real quick), and also in the human interest angle, namely which executioner has the bum cartridge in his breech. Throughout the nation there is a good deal of friendly wagering over this, and NEXXON has extracted a promise from Warden Boyd Earle to disclose which one.

Executioners hand in their rifles in turn, leave together. Only Four notices the beggar now outside the kill-yard, squatting on his hams in the fierce early sun, dazedly licking his fingers...Four points to the beggar but the others still do not see him. Four's cartridge is the bum one. The American people are not surprised. The television camera has a way of pinpointing things, and they saw this in him, in the way he wore his trousers, in the cast of his jaw.

Cameras and sound equipment mounted on trucks. Media people, shills, free-lancers have their final coffee and danish in Salt Lake City...

NEXXON's Capsule: "A viewer recently asked me: 'Mr. Nexxon, what is it that pointed you toward Communication, and once in your field, what is it that enabled you to rise to the very top?'

"I answered the question in this way: 'I communicate as well as I do because I have no tail to waggle.'

"The problem with G as we see it is that he had too much tail to waggle. And the same applies to the thousands of other recidivists and mindless felons who occupy our penal institutions and the inner city streets that spawn them."

VILE BODY, VIOLENT ART

VILE BODY, VIOLENT ART

August. Hot. New York City-sixth-circle-of-hell-hot. Smog, the babel whirr of air conditioning, hillocks of garbage fermenting on the sidewalks...

Rosen, nude, was sitting at his battered Olivetti in front of his study window. No air conditioner. Window gaping like an open grave (or a field of grain; depending on how Rosen's writing was progressing). Today and for several consecutive days it was an open grave: he had not written a single salvageable page in the last two weeks, and all he had done today was perspire onto the typewriter keys.

He banged the table with both fists, got up and paced about the room. For some reason—his agitation? the heat?—he became erect. One of those impertinent hard-ons (he often got them while marching in the army) which have nothing to do with the matter at hand. Rosen was about to sit down again at the typewriter when he noticed some-one in the building across the street. A woman sitting at her own open window was distinctly staring at his nudity. After a confused hesita-tion, Rosen went into his bedroom for his robe—when he came back she was gone.

Writing was obviously out of the question now. Rosen had a hur-ried shower and left the apartment. He ducked into the house across the street and scanned the names on the mailboxes. Eighteen boxes, no way to discover which one belonged to that window.

He decided to buy a book. Why not? In the process he could agonize a little over the fertility of his peers. Mortification might open some...

casements: consider the saints. Rosen was examining a Robbe-Grillet paperback in a neighborhood bookshop when it came to him: he would write about the window business.

Before going upstairs he dropped into the delicatessen on the corner. It was atypically crowded for that time, and as he was waiting for his turn to squeeze the avocados, he thought he saw *her* walk up to the counter with some packages. It looked like her, but he couldn't be sure since their windows were not close and he was nearsighted. She saw him but made no acknowledgement.

When in his apartment Rosen removed the few purchases from the paper bag, he found a note on a small piece of tissue. In pencil in a brazen fluent hand it read: "Beta He / Alpha She." That was all. Rosen went into the study and looked through the window. Her shade was lowered. Actually three of her windows faced him, two in her bedroom and one in what must have been her kitchen. All three shades were lowered.

At his typewriter Rosen began something which he entitled: "Beta He / Alpha She." Mostly he recapitulated what in fact had gone on, hoping that the thing would discover somehow its own inscape, take wing. A while later he got up—but then sat down again and altered the title to "Alpha He / Omega She."

The following morning someone was sitting—back facing out—on the windowsill of one of her bedroom windows, evidently washing it. Rosen put on his glasses. It looked like her wearing a loose dress and a kerchief on her head, but he wasn't certain. Possibly she lived with a roommate, or it might have been a cleaning-person. Straining his eyes Rosen made out what appeared to be a scrawl in large, cleansing-agent yellow letters on the top pane. As far as he could tell it said: PALP. Rosen reflected for a moment, then consulted his O.E.D. (abridged)...

"Palp." He searched in his closet for a pair of binoculars to confirm this curious word. He couldn't locate them, and when he looked through the window again she—or whoever it was—was washing the second bedroom window. Rosen fixed on her for several minutes. When she began to work on the inside portion of this window she faced him and then he was certain she was the woman he had seen in the delicatessen. She saw him staring at her—no question about that—but gave no sign.

When at last she finished with the windows, she immediately low-ered all the shades. "Alpha" crap! A manipulative jade rather, whose dumb show was to be enacted according to her rules—or not at all. Rosen at his Olivetti wrote that down. And then his mind began to work: he thought of several fantastic sequences to this "communica-tion" of theirs. He started to list these fantasies before he forgot them. The phone rang. It was in the bedroom, and when he picked it up on the third ring the party had already hung up.

At the typewriter again he glanced through the window and was not entirely surprised to see her nude behind her now open bedroom window, walking back and forth with something in her hand, perhaps a dust rag. Or was it a conch? Rosen considered lowering *his* shade, but that was her gambit; he would need to come up with his own. Besides, he wanted to look at her. She looked very good: dark-haired, slender, firm-breasted. He wondered whether she could be observed from other windows, whether she was displaying herself to others at the same time.

Scratching his large dry head, Rosen thought for a moment: his building had three tenants, and the couple beneath him had closed their apartment for the summer. The tenants of the building to his right, which was separated from him by a thick brick wall, would not be able to see into her window because their angle was too wide. To his left was the street. This peculiar geography, then, afforded them the privacy to carry on their communication. (Rosen wrote *that* down.)

That evening Rosen phoned R, who occasionally visited an acquaintance in her building. R was a sculptor, worked with steel. His left leg was several inches shorter than his right and he carried a medieval-looking wood and steel crutch; he had fashioned it himself. Rosen described her and told R where her windows were located. R phoned his contact then got back to Rosen. His man, R said, could think of only two possibilities: the names were Evans and Swirkhoff.

Rosen checked the directory; only Swirkhoff was listed. When he queried the operator she said that Evans had requested an unlisted number. Rosen moved his phone into the study. He sat at his type-writer for more than an hour, not writing, but waiting until he was certain he saw her in her bedroom. Immediately he dialed Swirkhoff's number: no one answered. The woman across the street would have to be Evans.

Rosen typed half a page then went into the living room and put a record on his record player: a vina recital from Kandy state, Sri Lanka. Vina and tamboura, the soulful drone. Music devoted to the godly crapulence of Lord Krishna. Ungainly Rosen removed his clothes and did his version of a sybaritic dance about his bookish living room. Then he took his Polaroid self-developer out of a drawer and snapped two photos of his penis, one detumescent, the other erect. He fitted each photo into an envelope which he sealed. When the record ended Rosen dressed and went across the street where he slipped the detumescent penis into Evans' box.

Rosen had a good many things to do the next day and didn't return until supper time. He noticed that all three of Evans' windows were covered. At half past midnight his telephone rang—it was R who, down on his luck as usual, asked for a loan.

The following morning Rosen wrote. When he went downstairs to get his mail he found a small white envelope, unsealed, in his mailbox. It was his photo, apparently returned—no, something else. She had cut off the tip of his penis with a pair of scissors—and then returned it...

That evening she was in front of her window, nude. Rosen looked at her for a while, then resumed writing with his window open. The following evening she was there again, but he continued writing, elaborating his...fiction, which engaged his interest as no writing had done for some time. The title he had changed once again to "Vile Body, Violent Art." It was nearly dawn when Rosen left his flat and slipped the second photo—penis erectus—into Evans' mailbox.

He did not see any sign of her for the next few days. He wondered whether she had gone away for the weekend. Tuesday morning he found an outsized envelope stuffed into his mailbox and opened it on the spot...With crayons and paper and paste she had fashioned a collage out of his photo. Rosen's penis sported a bird's beak, feathers and wings and was rising with desperate eyes out of a fiery nest.

Upstairs Rosen held up the collage (still moist with the sweet-smelling paste) alongside his face and gazed into the mirror. Uncanny! She had actually managed to capture his predominant expression. In the eyes.

She had guests that evening. Rosen saw several silhouettes through her lowered shades and heard her music, which, though it didn't sound especially loud to him some twenty-five meters away, was just persistent enough to interfere with his writing. At one point Evans raised her shade and pointed to Rosen's apartment: she and the two men next to her—one on either side—laughed. Rosen decided to phone the police about the excessive noise. They arrived within fifteen minutes, and soon he was able to work and, afterwards, sleep without the benefit of her music. It was unkind music. It was not the kind of music with which Rosen would net his lady.

The following morning Rosen listened to purple Krishna's surge and drone, while stroking his bird. Later he deposited the sticky sheath in Evans mailbox. His message read (he wondered whether too cryptically): "Alpha Phoenix Spits Fire."

It rained for the next three days. Rosen kept his window shade down and wrote. Meanwhile he had again contacted R and asked whether his man could furnish any additional information on Evans. That night the phone rang at 12:30 a.m., but when Rosen picked it up the party clicked off. He went back into his study, raised the shade, and saw Evans and a man—one of the two from her party night. They were nude and in profile. Evans, kneeling, had the crown of his penis in her mouth. She tilted her head toward Rosen while flashing him a cunning (and possibly contemptuous) look. Then the man, his "palp" still engaged, but with a curiously detached expression on his face, lowered the shade.

According to information he got from penurious R (Rosen naturally paid him for his trouble), Evans was a librarian, but had taken the summer, or most of it, off. Rosen's own surveillance indicated that her habits were irregular except for Thursday evenings, when she left her flat around 7:15 and returned sometime after 11. Evidently she was spending these hours in "group therapy." Rosen imagined her recounting her experiences with the loony coarse-haired writer in his window across the street. She supplied the sordid details in a sober, dutiful tone even as (beneath the table) she caressed her thigh. The five or six others—an account executive, a law student, a male nurse, a "producer" of TV documentaries, a buyer for Saks Fifth Avenue— listened with rapt, vacuous eyes. The psychotherapist, in bushy grey sideburns and desert boots, ground his wide hips against his chair and nodded his head. He knew; he had read all about it in Krafft-Ebing.

Suddenly, unaccountably, Rosen's writing started to bog down. The several pages he had completed were, he was convinced, strange, resonant. Yet somehow he had gotten derailed. He couldn't help but blame Evans. For more than a week now she had done nothing to incite his imagination. Not only did she seem to make a point of *not* appearing nude when her shades were raised—the shades were scarcely raised, even during the daylight hours.

This latest turn was not good. All Rosen needed was time, a little time to twist the knife. Two or three twists would do it. It would be done, he would be on track, his quivering palp would be inserted solidly in his echoing center...

Was there any compelling reason to draw back? No, there was not. That very night Rosen contacted R and explained his impasse. After a brief hesitation, R agreed to do Rosen's bidding for a substantial, though not unconscionable, fee, and the assurance that the risk he was taking was minimal. This was Tuesday. The following Thursday at 11:18 p.m., Evans was definitively raped in her own apartment. Nothing was stolen (except, that is, for a few items of lingerie). The rapist evidently entered the corridor from a stairwell just as she was opening the door to her flat. He switched on the light, raised the bedroom shades, forced her to kneel with her back to him and her elbows on the windowsill, and penetrated her in the pertinent orifices both with his penis and with a blunt-edged instrument of some kind, which—the victim was unclear here—might have been a cane or crutch. Evans did not herself report her violation to the police.

Yea, Rosen's writing was airborne—cradling the smoggy breeze very prettily, except that he could not decide which of these codas was most satisfactory:

1: When it was over, as Evans lay on her side in a state of partial shock, R slipped into her robin's-egg blue bikini panties and delicate fashioned-in-France bra and performed a queer dance or jig in front of her lighted window to the accompaniment of music—if you can call it that: staccato, heavily accented, punctuated by extended drones.

2: About six weeks later two policemen with search warrants entered Rosen's apartment, interrogated him about the rape, and when he pleaded ignorance, pillaged his manuscripts.

3: A few nights after this incident Rosen discovered Evans languid with heartache on the doorstep of his building. He helped her inside, bathed her, applied poultices to her forehead, and subsequently annexed her, altering her Christian name to "Harriet," introducing her into the circle of his dispossessed.

4: Evans' violation served only to inflame her deviant passion. Her bedroom shades were now nearly always raised, and when she wasn't cavorting with one or more men in full view, she was prancing about naked. Evans was striving; she had sacrificed nuance, grace. Rosen was constrained to write her off.

MOCTEZUMA'S DREAMER

MOCTEZUMA'S DREAMER

DREAM

Teshko: It is a just thing I have done as the God-Sun is my witness. Tomorrow dawn I am gone. It matters little. Before the completion of the next cycle the Empire itself will be gone. It is so. I have dreamed it.

Tomorrow dawn my Lord's High Priest will carve the incision in my breast and rip out my heart as offering. Neither my blood nor the blood of countless others will appease the dream. The very heart's-blood of the Empire will be sacrificed before a force fierce as the Sun, though rising in the west. Four times before in the life of the world it has happened, and this will mark the fifth, commencing the final end.

Lionel Bent's Gloss: Fifty-two year cycles constituted the major divisions in the Aztec calendar, and the end of each cycle was viewed with foreboding. In 1507, merely five years after Moctezuma had proclaimed himself Liege-Lord, one of the cycles ended and Moctezuma was the soul of gloom. In truth the signals were ominous. A severe drought had come upon the land destroying crops and grazing animals. This was immediately succeeded by extraordinary rains which overflowed the lakes and flooded the august burial mounds. As if these were not portent enough, a vast eruption in the skies ignited several huge fires in the central temples. Moctezuma called for his dreamer, captured from the Colhuacán, Teshko, who had served him long, who had dreamed his ascent.

Teshko: The dream uttered, my Lord's great gloom was confirmed. Soon, then, the dreamer will be gone. The dream-center will be ripped from my breast as offering to the God-Sun. It cannot be undone. Nor will the high-born, blending my limbs' marrow in their piquant stews, sup much longer. I have dreamed it.

Bent: Teshko relinquished his heart. His severed skull was added to the hundreds of thousands. His excised limbs contributed to the lords' protein. The burnished white raptor rose out of the west obscuring the sun. The final ending commenced. The heart's dream will not die.

AUGURY

In the process of making his way south, Lionel Bent sojourned here and there en route looking for auspices. When, a few months before he left the U.S., an acquaintance had mentioned that a certain Q, an anthropologist from Stanford, was living and studying the practices of a Cakchiquel shaman in Chac Mool, Guatemala, Bent made a note. When he arrived in Guatemala he bussed to Chac Mool, a small pueblo perched on a slope of the cordillera in the southwest, bisected by the Tecún River. The Cakchiquel were Maya, but in the view of at least two historians they were also racially connected to the Colhuacán, the dreamer Teshko's people.

Q was one of those delicately constituted but determinedly rugged field anthropologists. He was a little drunk when Bent located him sitting as a calloused cantina table drinking kush, the coarse highland liquor. According to Q, Don Pez, his shaman (or *zahorin,* the local term) informant, with whom he had lived for three years, though but one of half a dozen shamans in Chac Mool, was the "most powerful and refined" of all of them. Q reminded Bent that *pez* in Spanish meant "fish"; accordingly Don Pez's *nagual*-familiar was the ouzel, a bird that is a strong flier but that feeds by walking along the floor of the Tecún River.

Among the services Don Pez performed were divinations with beans, ritualistic blessings (called *costumbres*), and healings by means of herbs. Before Bent had an opportunity to broach the subject, Q suggested that Bent join Don Pez and himself the following evening at another cantina across the river.

Bent did this, making his way through the narrow, twisting paths, over the rickety log bridge which spanned the river. When the Indians became noticeably drunk in unruly clusters he knew he was almost there. Don Pez and Q stood at the counter of the cramped store-front cantina with space on either side of them (the *pobres,* Bent learned, always gave a wide berth to the *zahorin*). Q had said that Don Pez was close to seventy. He looked much younger: coarse, slate-colored hair, the granite hawk profile, not wearing *traje* (the tribal costume) as most of the Chac Mool natives did, but a stained, misshapen stetson tilted back on his head, gringo shirt, trousers, tire-soled sandals. In response to Bent's formally respectful greeting, the *zahorin* turned to him his left eye. It was a rheumy, boozy eye—yet the glance was penetrating.

Q handed Bent a bottle of beer. He and Don Pez were drinking kush. They—Q and the *zahorin*—drank and talked (in Spanish and Cakchiquel) for the next four hours. Don Pez seemed relaxed, languid, possibly drunk, apparently not ill-disposed to Bent's being there. However he said nothing at all to Bent until the cantina was closing and they were ready to separate. "You wish divination?" he inquired, fixing Bent with his keen left eye. Bent hesitated just slightly before saying that he did. "*Muy bien.* Day after tomorrow is best moon. Come at sunset."

Walking back across the river through the gauntlets of drunk Indians, Lionel Bent witnessed an old man vomit his kush and tortillas and two outcast dogs rush to the mess snapping at each other, lapping it up.

Laden with four quart bottles of kush and eight packets of native cigarettes as well as fifteen *quetzales,* and accompanied by Q who meant to observe, Bent appeared at Don Pez's compound at the appointed time. The *zahorin*'s conjuring hut (or *cueva,* as it was called) was constructed of mud and brick and was roughly iglooshaped; it stood ten or fifteen meters east of the larger wooden structure in which he lived. The entire compound smelled strongly of the copal incense which issued from the *cueva.* Q and Bent removed their shoes and entered through the low opening. In the flickering light of several candles Don Pez was kneeling at a small altar arranging the ritualistic wood and clay figures. The earthen floor was strewn with fresh pine needles; fragrant cypress branches were affixed to the walls. In the center of the floor a ceramic brazier of copal incense was smoking. Q motioned Bent to squat with him against the wall. After a time Don Pez took Bent's cigarettes, broke open two packets and shredded them into the smoking copal.

For the divination that followed Don Pez used a particular *frijole* (the same black bean, Q said afterwards, that his shaman Maya ancestor had used), and the words he uttered combined Proto-Maya, Cakchiquel and Spanish. While Don Pez and Bent kneeled on their right knees, the *zahorin* held a lighted candle in his hand and speaking into it as if it were a microphone, gave thanks first to *U Kush Kah, U Kush Uleu,* "The Heart of the Sky, The Heart of the Earth." Next he thanked *Jesucristo;* his familiar, the ouzel; and at the far end of the altar away from the other icons: *El Otro,* the devil.

The beans were kept in a sacramental silver box, circular in shape and enfolded in a section of tapestry etched with hieratic symbols from the Maya calendar. With a deft motion Don Pez overturned the box onto the altar and scooped up beans with each hand. Turning to the far left corner of the altar to the clay figure of *El Otro,* Don Pez paid the obligatory though grudging respects in a guttural Spanish, depositing his left fistful of beans in front of this personage. Then, invoking the benign spirit of the ouzel on the opposite end of the altar, he laid out his right handful of beans in clusters of four.

In nearly every instance (Q was to explain) there are one or two or three beans left over in the final cluster; for Bent the clusters not only came out evenly, but there were twelve of them. This was an unusually high number since the average was nine or ten. Don Pez himself seemed surprised, said something to Q, gathered up the beans with his right hand, returned them to the large pile, then took up a handful again (using all but his smallest finger) and laid them out on the altar a second time. The result was identical: twelve clusters of beans, none left over. Again the *zahorin* spoke to Q.

Q explained: "Don Pez feels there is something powerful here and wishes to begin the *costumbre* at once so that he can find out what it is." "Wasn't Don Pez going to do a *costumbre* anyway?" Bent questioned. "Yes, but later after a good deal of preparation. Now he wants to get right into it..."

While Q and Bent squatted against the wall Don Pez lighted more candles, rearranged the altar so that the ouzel occupied the centermost position, added copal pellets and cigarette tobacco to the smoking brazier...Then kneeling on his right knee and facing his familiar he took a long swig of kush, passed the bottle to Q who drank and handed it to Bent who took a short drink and gave the bottle back to Don Pez; the *zahorin* swigged again then poured some of the alcohol onto the incense and tobacco. The fire spit, the smoke snaked up thickly. Bent, coughing and rubbing his eyes, could scarcely see. When the smoke cleared a litle he saw that the *zahorin* held the clay ouzel in his right hand and was speaking into it as he had into the candle. When he stopped speaking his right leg twitched violently—as if in response. He spoke again, paused, his leg twitched, he swigged kush, passed the bottle, fanned the fire. This sequence continued for a few hours at least. Bent, drunk and thick-headed, had largely lost track of time.

Afterwards, outside the *cueva* under a yellow, implausible moon, Don Pez spoke earnestly, feelingly to the tipsy Bent, several times gesturing to the ouzel which he still held in his hand. When he finished he embraced Bent, pulling him close to his chest. The old Indian smelled of smoke and liquor and incense and his unexpected embrace was so reassuring that Lionel Bent didn't want to be released.

Walking back across the river Q said: "Did you understand what Don Pez was saying?" "Not really. Too much kush." Q laughed. "Your beans said power. That was clear. But Don Pez wasn't certain about the nature of this power. The *costumbre* cleared it up. You saw his right leg twitching?" "Yes." "That is a good sign. If it were his left leg or certain other parts of his body it wouldn't have been good. This right-left thing with the Maya goes way back, it long precedes the duality system of Zoroastrianism, for example." "Interesting," Bent said. "Yes. And ordinarily Don Pez doesn't address his *nagual* in the *costumbre*. Sometimes he addresses *El Otro,* or *Jesucristo,* or one of the saints. But in your instance the ouzel was essential because according to Don Pez your power is in the dream; this is the aspect of the ouzel that flies high above the cliffs of the cordillera. But flying continually will fatigue and ultimately destroy you unless you alternate it with the kind of living that other people do. This is the other aspect of the ouzel, the water. Though you are a different species from nearly all those who surround you, you must walk with them, feed with them, weep with them beneath the water. And you must soar."

ART

It is February. Lionel Bent, en route to Tierra del Fuego, has been living in Guayaquil, Ecuador, for nearly a month. For the last eleven

days he has shared a cage with Pato, the day man. Bent is nightclerk at
Hotel Berlin, a runty, ill-maintained structure on the Guayas River.
This is the same river on which the ancient Quechua sailed when he
made his way southeast ahead of the ice sheet, across the Bering land
bridge...

Like any seaport town Guayaquil has its *maleantes*—thieves, murderers, pimps, touts, pickpockets. Each of these genres is represented
at Hotel Berlin. Bent observes them from his bulletproof cage. In
broken Spanish he occasionally services them in his capacity of nightclerk.

Pato, the experienced day man, advises: "Never mind who they
are—they pay you, you rent them the room."

Bent is obliged to do this in spite of the more than occasional incivil-
ity that results. Tonight though something more happened. It looked
like homicide though Bent could not be certain.

A Bolivian sailor on a day's pass picked up one of the local pros-
titutes and rented a room from nightclerk Bent, paying with Bolivian
pesos. The young sailor signed the register as "Tupac," which Bent
recognized as a Proto-Quechua name. Indeed the sailor with his slim
build, coppery hue and delicate hawklike features looked to be a
full-blooded Quechua.

Less than an hour after the boy followed his Latina prostitute up the
stairs, Bent heard a muffled (his cage was largely soundproof) uproar
and witnessed darting down the stairs: the prostitute in her platform
heels, her hair in disarray, behind her the young Quechua wearing his
sailor cap and nothing else. An artificial jacaranda tree stood in the
center of the run-down lobby, and the distraught boy actually chased
her round and around the tree—not catching her...

Bent witnessing, but scarcely hearing from within his elevated glass
cage, thought at once of the "Ghost Dance," that phenomenon which
began among the North American Paiutes and rapidly spread across
the plains and subsquently into Central and South America. The dance
consisted of a a ceremonial circling about a pole which resembled the
maypole, though its moral affinity (so to speak) was to that great ash
linking heaven and earth: Yggdrasil. The naked and bereft Indian boy
pursuing his light-skinned oppressor was appropriate, since the dual
intention of the Ghost Dance was to exorcise the white devil while
reviving the spirit of the departed Red.

That's how the mute scene struck Bent. The resemblance was
enforced when (as in a dumb-show) the girl's pimp bolted in through

the outside door, pursued the Quechua around the tree, caught him, stabbed him between the shoulders.

Others, street people, had by now flooded into the hotel. The naked boy lay sprawled on his stomach with the long, intricately figured knife handle protruding from the center of his back, beneath the artificial tree. Pimp and girl fled. Lionel Bent was about to dial the notoriously inept Guayaquil police, when two of them, mustachioed, with the low-down look of Alabama deputy sheriffs, swaggered into the hotel with their archaic .45 calibers holstered low on their hips.

CHRISTMAS BIRD COUNT

(for J.G.)

CHRISTMAS BIRD COUNT

Dawn. At Butter lane we heard a faint rhyhmic tapping punctuate the mist, then spotted a male downy (*Dendrocopus pubescens*) on the trunk of a dead hornbeam fronting Swan Creek. Rosen wrote it down. Not a bad way to start. Swan Creek itself was void. "Not even a crummy mallard," Rosen whined. "No, but look there," I pointed into the rising sun. "Look at that—a loon." Rosen whispered. "Red-throated loon," I said. "*Gavia stellata*. Write it down."

We got back into the Chrysler. Rosen turned to me. His nose was dripping from the cold. "Where do you think he is, Duane?" "Keep your eye on the road," I said. "I'm just wondering where he is, that's all." "We'll watch for his bug," I said. Rosen, sardonically: "You mean he didn't take his motorcycle?" "I doubt it. A BMW 760 is not really suitable for birding. But then Klaus will surprise you," I joked. Rosen gave me a dark look.

The mist was lifting. We headed west on Horsemill Lane, then turned south on Ocean Road. Two mourning doves were perched on a telephone wire. As I added them to Rosen's list I whistled: "Oh little town of—" "For God's sake, don't!" Rosen hissed.

Sagaponack lake flows northeast from the ocean. Bordering the lake on the east is a wood. Parking the Chrysler there we heard a small well-tuned engine and turned in time to see Klaus's yellow bug purr by us going south. Rosen frowned. "Where's he going? To the ocean?" "Looks like it." "What's there besides herring gulls and maybe a tern or two?" I shrugged. We entered the wood.

"Smells good." "What do you mean, Duane?" 'Clover,' I said. "Can't you smell it?" "All I smell is smoke—" I held my hand up, we listened. "Catbird," Rosen whispered. "Two of them," I whispered. We continued to listen. "You're right, Duane. I wonder what kept these from going south." "Pokeweed." Rosen looked at me reproachfully. "Pokeweed," I repeated. *Phytolacca americana*. It's a shrub in the holly family. Catbirds like the berries." "How many you think he's got, Duane?" "Klaus, you mean. Hard to tell. He's a darn good birder. Has a good pair of ears." "That's from listening to so much Bruckner." "Don't be so gloomy, Rosen. Klaus is alone. You've got me." Immediately Rosen's expression changed: he looked shamed. "I know I do, Duane. Why did you come with me anyway?" I laughed. "To make up for the handicap. You against Klaus would be no contest, would it?" This produced in Rosen his aggrieved look—which was interrupted by the brief whirr of a small bird landing in front of us on an American bittersweet. Another whirr, another...and then the familiar five note scolding call of the black-capped chickadee. They wanted to be fed. "I wish I had remembered the sunflower seeds," Rosen chided himself. "I count five," I said. "There's another. Six chickadees, partner."

The wood merged with a potato farm which we traversed diagonally until we came out on Bridge Road. Seven or eight starlings passed us overhead. *"Sturnus vulgaris,"* Rosen recited somberly. I grinned: "Right. The Puerto Ricans of birds. Eight of them."

Back in the Chrysler I said, "What is this between you and Klaus, Rosen?" Rosen turned his black exophthalmic eyes to me appraisingly. Then he emitted a heavy premonitory sigh—but I held up a hand. "Never mind, partner. Don't say anything. It's none of my business. I shouldn't have asked."

"Turn left there, Rosen. Meadowlark Lane." I consulted my map. "We should hit Little Long Pond on the northeast just down the way, maybe two hundred meters." Behind the wheel Rosen's dry dark head was heavy with gloom. "Cheer up, you're doing real good so far." He turned to me his doubting right eye. "Am I, Duane?"

Two oldsquaws and three buffleheads were in the pond, and in the southernmost tip were two mute swans, one a juvenal. Rosen wrote it all down. We were standing behind a thick-trunked red maple, studying the scene through binoculars. "I've known him for a long time," Rosen remarked apropos of nothing and without lowering his binoculars. "Klaus, I mean. Not him personally, Duane. But his kind. I was born on the other side, you know. There were a lot of Klauses there. Too many."

We remained in the area of Little Long Pond for nearly seventy minutes and spotted a sharp-shinned hawk, a male and four female ring-necked pheasants, a bobwhite, a red-breasted nuthatch creeping headfirst down a cedar, a couple dozen canada geese, and four bewhiskered ravens (*Corvus corax*).

"This 'other side' you mentioned, partner. Where you were born. I suppose Advent was celebrated there as well?" "Advent? I don't understand, Duane." "I mean beginnings, Rosen. New beginnings." After a minute he said somberly: "Yes, that was part of it. These Klauses all wanted to have their new beginnings. Golden dawn is what they sometimes called it."

Rosen brought his heavy-boned wrist to his face. "It's ten-thirty, Duane. Are you hungry?" "Not much. Here, have some raisins." "I would suggest we stop for breakfast," Rosen continued. "There's a diner not more than a mile from here. But I know that Klaus will just go right on birding. He'll probably go right on till dusk without stopping. I don't want to give him that edge." "Why not, partner?" "Why not what?" "Why is it so important that he not get this 'edge'?" Rosen lowered his binoculars and fixed me with his queer assessor's gaze. I continued to peer through my binoculars at a distant clump of locusts where I had seen something stir, possibly a black-crowned night heron.

When we left Little Long Pond and were driving slowly west, parallel to the ocean, we heard Klaus's yellow bug, then saw it as it overtook us and turned north on Whooping Hollow Path. As he turned Klaus honked his horn, as if in greeting. Rosen's nervousness increased. He shook his head. "You know Klaus fairly well, don't you, Duane?" "I suppose so." "Where did you meet him—if you don't mind my asking?" "I met him at a convocation." "At a convocation?" "That's right, partner. At a convocation for concerned citizens." After a short silence Rosen said, "I see."

"What do you see, Rosen?" We were looking south athwart a meadow to the ocean. We could see whitecaps beyond the shore; dimly, we could hear the surf. "A predator, Duane. A marsh hawk, it looks like. Circling low over the meadow, above those pines." 'They're spruce, not pine, partner. Is there white on its rump?" "Can't tell, but it's behaving like a marsh hawk." I glanced through my binoculars. "You're right. *Circus cyaneus.*" I lowered my glasses. "Anything else?" "Herring gulls, Duane. I guess that's what they are. Four or five way out there. Over the ocean." I studied Rosen's profile and thick brow as he gazed through his binoculars. "They're predators, too," I said Rosen lowered his binoculars, turned to me. "What do you mean?" I laughed. "Herring gulls are predators. *Larus argentatus.* So is that fish crow—do you see it there to the east, flapping? You're surrounded by predators, partner."

"How many do you have, Rosen?" It was two-fifteen. "Thirty-one species. A total," he computed, "of 118 birds." "Not bad," I said. "What are the criteria?" "Criteria?" Rosen repeated. "Right. Between you and Klaus. I assume species counts more than overall number." We were walking along the ocean from west to east. The wind from the northeast bit, the surf was breaking hard. "Don't you know what the rules are, Duane?" "How would I know?" I shouted. "I don't even know what the stakes are. Judging by the way you look I'd guess they were pretty high." "What do you mean, the way I look?" Rosen shouted. "You look gloomy, partner. And scared," I shouted. "You look about scared enough to shit."

At five minutes to three we stopped at that small diner Rosen had mentioned and bought some sandwiches and coffee which we ate in the Chrysler, parked across from the Poxabogue Golf Course on Parson's Lane. "I've never birded on a golf course without seeing at least one kildeer," I said. "Look there, Rosen. Kildeer, male. *Charadrius vociferus.*" As Rosen was writing this down I said, "That's a short thumb you have there, partner." Rosen glanced at me, then at the short blunt thumb that was squeezing his pencil stub...

In the Chrysler: "The reason I might seem nervous is this is my first Christmas bird count, you know." "I know, partner. And you're doing swell. You're doing real good." "Thanks. I thought I knew my birds, but I'm really a novice next to you, Duane. When did you first develop your interest in birds?" "When?" "Yes. I'm just curious." "At about the same time that Klaus did," I said. "In the same place actually. That concerned citizens' convocation I mentioned." "You studied birds in this convocation, Duane?" "We did calisthenics. We exchanged ideas. We did other things. And we studied birds, yes. I'll tell you something else, partner: Klaus is blond all over." Rosen seemed surprised: "Blond all over?" I grinned: "That's what I said."

As we were driving north on Alewife Brook Road we flushed a sparrow hawk who had been perched on a wire tearing at a vole. It flew away with the remains of its meal secure in is talons. "Another predator for you," I said. Rosen, who had stopped the Chrysler, was already taking it down. "You seem to enjoy saying 'predator' to me, Duane." "I enjoy seeing predators, partner. Don't you?" This was received in silence. Until several minutes later as we were moving toward Crooked Lane. Rosen said, "What is it about predators that attracts you? I'm just curious." "Obviously, Rosen. Otherwise you wouldn't ask the question, would you? Your predator is fierce, he is a meat-eater, and he is single-minded. I like the obsessive focus of his gaze. I'm talking about eagles and hawks now. Falcons, harriers, *buteos*. I don't mean gulls or crows. To be honest with you, partner, there's not a single thing I don't like about your true predator."

"There goes your Chrysler, Rosen." The generator light flashed, the car coughed...and died. We were in the middle of Mecox Road. "Oh shit!" Rosen moaned. "Do you know anything about cars, Duane?" I laughed. "I'm a white male Protestant, aren't I? I doubt that it's your battery. It could be your voltage regulator. Or the generator itself. It'll be dark in less than two hours. I don't know what to tell you, partner."

I said, "We have only one major stop left anyway, Rosen. Sagg Swamp Sanctuary. And we could walk to it from here. It's no more than half a mile southeast." "But what about my car?" "When we're done maybe Klaus'll give you a lift to a service station," I said. Rosen shook his head, no. I shrugged: "You're not going to add to your count sitting here brooding." Rosen banged both fists on the wheel, then followed me out.

We walked the half-mile at a rapid pace. Away from the wind it wasn't cold. I sang, "At dusk I roam / ready to tear up the world / I roam—" "What's that?" Rosen demanded. "It's a Shinnecock hawk song," I said. "This was all Indian land at one time. You yourself have a special bond with these Indians, Rosen. In spite of your fear of predators. Certain ethnologists think that the eastern woodland Indians are related to the lost tribes of Zion. The Jew as Indian. You never came across this theory, partner?"

Not far from the entrance to the swamp on Crooked Lane a yellow bug was parked. "Klaus," Rosen whispered. I nodded. Fifteen or twenty meters into the sanctuary I held up a hand. "Listen..." A quavering whistle of about eight notes, descending. "An owl," Rosen whispered. "A screech owl. *Otus asio,* partner. Write it down. Maybe we'll see it. Keep an eye out for fur pellets. Especially near the box-elders. Can you recognize a box-elder?" "I don't think so. Not without its leaves. You seem to know this swamp, Duane."

We were moving deliberately and silently as we could through the dead leaves, over the marshy soil. Twice more we heard the screech owl's whistle. We saw no sign of it.

It was becoming stickier underfoot. I pushed aside the broken wooden gate. "It's wet here, isn't it?" Rosen said. "This is where the swamp proper begins," I said. "Keep your eye open for snipe." "It's wet. I don't think I'm wearing the proper shoes, Duane." I put my finger to my lips. "Do you hear it?" I whispered. "No." "Listen." "You mean that buzzing sound?" "Not buzzing, partner. Rasping. Listen...Now it's stopped. Common snipe. *Capella gallinago.* Write it down."

"Never mind your shoes. This swamp is crucial to your count." Rosen nodded somberly. "What was Klaus's car doing parked outside, Duane?" "Why, Klaus is here. In the swamp. I thought you knew that, partner." "Here?" "Right. The Christmas count for this area always concludes in Sagg Swamp. It's protocol." After a pause Rosen said, "That's an odd word to use, Duane. 'Protocol'."

Rosen paused. "What's that?" I gave Rosen a toothy grin. "Squirrels in the alders. They're rutting. Always do around Christmas. Or Chanukah—to use your language. You see that log?" "We don't have to ford that wet area, do we, Duane? It's kind of narrow." "Whose prints are those, Rosen?" I pointed to the swampy area on our side of the log. "Not Klaus's?" "Of course, Klaus's. That's his L.L. Bean Maine Hunting boot. Size 11." Rosen was looking at my feet. "That's right, partner, same kind as I wear. The best all-around boot you can buy. Just take your finger out of your ass and concentrate. And keep your knees bent. You'll make it." Rosen looked at me doubtfully. "What's on the other side, Duane?" "Several species, if we're lucky. Ever hear of the jewbird? *Coprophag migratorius*? Only kidding. you go first, partner. It's just a bit viscous. Wouldn't want you to go under…"

The last image I had was of Rosen's large sopping head and doomed exophthalmic eyes beneath my L.L. Bean boot. "See you at Easter, partner."

Not far from where Rosen went down Klaus was sprawled languidly under a pignut hickory sucking on a reed. He gave me his sideways smile. "Guess I won, huh?" "You won all right." I held up my hand. "Do you hear that burbling?" We both turned to the swamp—a mild agitation on the surface, bubbles. We looked into each other's eyes. *"Coprophag migratorius,"* Klaus said with mock solemnity, knitting his brow. I slapped my thigh and laughed.

The BMW 760 was waiting for us on Crooked Lane. It started at once. Klaus, behind me, cradled my waist.

PART II

comrades
you fled
even the eagle dies

(Teton Sioux)

COPROLALIA

COPROLALIA

Elk Mole, a Lakota Sioux, was on a drunk. Together with three reservation buddies, he finished potato picking just after sundown on Saturday, picked up his bimonthly pay from the foreman's shack, washed up in the pickers' trough, and headed for the first Lakota bar he came to, which was about fifty meters south of the foreman's shack.

Elk Mole and the brothers bought rounds in turn. They started with bourbon and beer chasers, switched to rye with beer chasers, and were into their fourth round of beer with rye chasers, when the bar closed for the night. It was 3:30 a.m. One brother said he had drunk enough and was going back to the reservation to get some sleep. Elk Mole and the two others hadn't drunk enough; they walked the two miles into Silt River and bore down on the all-night whiteman's bar by the railroad. Just two people inside: the bartender and a whiteman drinker, both snoring with their heads on the counter. Awakened by the noisy Lakotas, the bartender took their dollars and set two quart bottles of bourbon on the counter...

At 7:00 a.m., as the church bells were clanging, the Indians killed the last of the bourbon. Their money was gone. One of the brothers had passed out. Elk Mole didn't want to stop drinking, but he knew enough not to ask for credit from the whiteman bartender.

They left the bar, laid the passed-out brother on a bank on the far side of the railroad, and stumbled off in the direction of the reservation. The last brother hung in there for about a mile, then collapsed. Elk Mole dragged him away from the road and laid him beneath a red willow, a secure place since it is from the bark of this tree that the Lakota makes the tobacco for the sacred pipe.

Elk Mole made it to the reservation, though not quite to his hut. He gave out as he got to the vision pit in the southeastern corner of the reservation next to the sacred sweat lodge. The vision pit was reserved for *pejuta wicasas,* medicine men; or for *heyokas,* the laughing thunder-dreamers. Elk Mole was of course neither of these; he was a part-time potato picker, quarry worker, gravedigger, drinker. And the only reason he didn't do this last full-time was money.

Elk Mole had nothing left. He toppled into the pit like a small tree. And it is at this juncture that the narrative becomes cloudy. What is clear is that Elk Mole was not discovered until two nights later by a *pejuta wicasa* who was undergoing preparation for the summer solstice. At first the *pejuta* thought that Elk Mole was dead. He was naked and there were bruises and claw marks all over his body. Evidently he had been attacked by a bear; the *pejuta* said he had smelled bear in the pit, and droppings were on the ground nearby. Why the bear attacked him without killing him, and how it was that Elk Mole's clothes disappeared, were but two of the questions that subsequently puzzled the reservation elders. More significantly, Elk Mole had been found in the vision pit four (the crucial number) days before the summer solstice, and though apparently dead, had been revived by the joint efforts of two *pejutas* and two *heyokas* after many hours.

Elk Mole's wounds were dressed and he was put to sleep in the chief *pejuta's* hut, where he remained until the solstice Sun Dance. This ancient and powerful ceremony which tested the faith and endurance of its participants, Elk Mole observed from a privileged place. It was four days since he was revived as if from the dead, and he had not yet uttered a syllable. Some of the brothers who had drunk with him and worked with him whispered together that he had changed, that he did not truly resemble the Elk Mole they had known.

The first words Elk Mole spoke were in response to a question put to him by the chief *pejuta's* daughter, who inquired whether he was hungry.

Elk Mole's response was: "Motherfucking fuck."

The girl paused. She wasn't certain she had heard correctly, but she didn't repeat her question. Instead she sent her younger brother to fetch their father. He came.

"I asked Elk Mole whether he was hungry and he answered me strangely."

The *pejuta* turned to Elk Mole. "You are feeling better, my son?"

"Long duck's cunting fuck," Elk Mole replied.

The *pejuta* turned to his daughter, then back to Elk Mole. He reflected for a moment before saying: "Why does the frail and precarious heron's nest set us to dreaming of security?"

"Long duck's cunting fuck," Elk Mole said again, the words hurtling out of his lips.

Again the *pejuta* paused. He said, "Nod your head if you heard the words that you just spoke."

Elk Mole didn't nod his head.

"Nod your head if you did not hear the words you spoke in response to my question."

Elk Mole did not nod his head. Nor did his expression waver. In fact his face was expressionless, as if he was in a trance.

The *pejuta* placed his hand on Elk Mole's shoulder, then kneaded the back of his neck. His hand slid down Elk Mole's spine. "I think you are much better," the *pejuta* said. "Do you feel pain?"

"Fucking motherfucking fuck."

It was concluded that Elk Mole was a *heyoka*. The *heyoka* is a holy fool or clown who receives his vision in a violent way, and is thus also called a thunder-dreamer. The *heyoka* always does unexpected or crazy things which are designed first to make people laugh, and then, on reflection, to remind that nature is forever fresh, vital, unpredictable, that it should never be taken for granted.

Elk Mole was a *heyoka* then, but even among this strange breed he was unusual, since every one of his utterances was an obscenity. Sometimes the obscenity was repeated, other times it was entirely new, and often the obscene words were strung together in eccentric combinations. The elders and *pejutas* and some of the more orthodox *heyokas* endeavored to discover a pattern in his responses: numerological, syllabic, anagrammatic...Most of them felt certain that a pattern of some kind existed, which once discerned would enable them to understand and subsequently act upon Elk Mole's responses.

The pattern eluded them.

ii

There exists a "relative" of Elk Mole who is (was) a white American. Call him Mole. Mole moved from job to job: was a Peace Corps volunteer in northwest Africa; did some government work with the U.S. Information Agency. Leaving that, he went to graduate school and took a doctorate in Clinical Psychology. For the next few years he administered psychotherapy in a federal prison, a state prison and in a state mental institution—all in the Camden-Philadelphia area. Approximately midway through his employment at the state prison he began to make critical statements about the prison administration which soon enough expanded into derogatory statements about the state government. Obviously this was intolerable and Mole was dismissed. In the mental institution the sequence was much the same as in the prison, but accelerated. Mole was one of three full-time clinical psychologists on the staff, and in a matter of months he had chosen to side with a dozen of the most refractory patients against his two colleagues and the hospital administration. What did he want? In order to get to what Mole actually wanted, it was necessary to penetrate his tedious diatribes about lack of professional compassion, insufficient patient responsibility, over-reliance on drug therapy, and the rest of it. When I and others expressed our impatience with his hair-trigger anarchism, he became belligerent. We not only dismissed him, we succeeded in revoking his New Jersey license and even initiated a procedure to void his affiliation with the American Psychological Association. Did it work? Yes, he was voided. What he did next was "counsel" draft-dodgers and war-resisters (this was in 1970). I don't know how he got paid for this, but one can imagine. He was involved with that leftist minister or ex-minister Dellinger, and I seem to recall that he even went to Cuba for some reason. Mole, that is. He obviously didn't have any coherent political philosophy, but every once in a while he made a statement that the media seized upon, and it was always belligerent and usually abusive. Inevitably protesters—most of them—grow up, protest goes out of vogue. In a couple of years Mole was out of work. The only two states where he could administer psychotherapy regardless of his APA discreditation were South Dakota and Florida. A reasonable professional wishing to get back on-track would, one expects, go to some urban or quasi-urban center in Florida and resume making a living. Mole went to Wounded Knee, South Dakota, and promptly got mixed up with the reservation militants. Rosebud Sioux, I think they were. I can't say what all he did there. I mean professionally. Maybe he counseled them, chewed peyote buttons with them, or got drunk with them. More likely he bent their ear about anarchism, since it couldn't have been more than a year after he got there that this Wounded Knee uprising took place. Some people died there, you may recall. And Mole himself was beaten up pretty good—he claims by the federal marshals, though others said it was the Sioux themselves who turned on him. In any case, he suffered some brain damage (partial left brain aphasia), which however didn't prevent him from lecturing the courtroom when he was tried several months later. The same rant he had always spouted, and it made things worse than they might have been—he was given fifteen months. Even at this juncture he could have negotiated for a suspended sentence, but of course he stubbornly refused to. He was put away in some federal institution—in Michigan, as I recall. And I'm sure I needn't have to say that once inside he began to proselytize and criticize and quote his Marxists and Buddhists and Gnostics. Yes, Gnostics. He was like a grave robber, coming up with stuff any other civilized human would consider immaterial, and which he distorted in any case. His point was that these Gnostics were supposed to have been the true Christians whose teachings resembled Buddhism and who were murdered or exiled by the Church Fathers. Okay, he did his time, was let go—and went right back to Wounded Knee. But the radicals there had meanwhile concluded that they couldn't battle what was larger than them and so weren't about to buy Mole's rant a second time. At this point Mole should have kept going west until he hit Calcutta, India, where he could have worked with the lepers. He could have talked his crap all day to them since they wouldn't understand his language and anyhow would accept a rupee from the devil himself if he offered it. Instead Mole turned around and made for Newark where he mucked around with the black militants who, among other things, were at odds with the Mafia-involved ward heelers. If you anticipate that Mole was finally about to shoot his wad, you're right. One evening he gave a hell-raising, cliché-ridden speech at a black community center regarding some gerrymandering plan which would give more power to the black majority. That night he was found dead in a ditch a few miles away. He had been shot four times in the head and neck, his tongue had been cut out of his mouth and pinned to his chest with a sign which read:

MOLE HE CUNT SHUT UP!

iii

Black, huge, female. Find her in the bus terminal, train terminal, public toilet. Massive soft shell in her elephant dress or shift, tattered oar-like shoes on archless feet. Tell her: "Drag your mammoth black ass out of here!" she won't answer, won't move. Some cop tells her this, she moves all right—but soon as he's gone she comes right back.

Huge and black and female. Hard to tell her age. Thirty-five? Twenty-eight? Forty-five? Her name is Birdie. Sprawl-seated in the terminal waiting room encompassed by commuters, she hums or sings or talks to herself in the third person: "Birdie don ax you no favor. You ain got no respek fuh her—gaw haid git out..." Disrespect, betrayal: the twin themes of her discourse, which is personal, even intimate, though—through her method—distanced. Her voice is more suited to her appearance than her name—a rich, full mezzo.

This is not the voice the commuters hear. In the bus terminal they are largely black, in the train terminal white. The tense whites are vexed, but only a little frightened because of their number, the fact that they are in a public place, the apparent fact that she is a woman. The whites hear obscenities, or something comparable, uttered in a discordant black person's voice. The blacks hear a crazy person who can't really not have—since she so damn fat. They pay her no mind.

"Birdie seed you look at yo watch then look at her. She ain did nuffin tuh you. Wifall de money an shit you got, what you wan fum Birdie?" (This in the train terminal.) "He done quit on her—jive muvva. Din say nuffin bout no other bitch neither..." (In the bus terminal.)

In the public toilet Birdie washes her hands. When she squats in the stall she reads the graffiti, moving her head down, up, sideways, lip-synching the words, sometimes singing the words.

It's always winter in this city and Birdie don't like the cold. On the rare uncold day she moves up out of her terminal, goes outside, shambles from one people cluster to another, keeps an eye out for dogs. She don't like dogs. Whenever Birdie moves out of her terminal she looks at store windows. Partly she looks at what there is in the window, mostly she looks at her own dim reflection and what's behind her. Like dogs.

Birdie will walk around the streets some. But not far. She don't like to walk too far. Less there's some reason for it. A parade's a reason if the drums sound nice. Three or four times Birdie's followed a parade, with the snare drums making a nice rattling sound. A person is sometimes a reason too. Sometimes Birdie will follow a person just like she follows a parade.

Tonight. No moon and dim, maybe snow in the air, but not real cold.

Birdie has taken up after a dwarf. Or almost-dwarf. Real small, sort of humped on the left side, with a large head and black, wide-apart eyes set deep in his head. Birdie had seen him twice before in the bus terminal (though he is a white dwarf) but had not followed him out because it was cold. Tonight she sees him behind her in the window of a greeting card store.

When he back away she follow him to Ninth Avenue where he approach by a dude wif a fucked-up foot. The dwarf seem to know him, he talk some words wif him, then hand him sumfin fum his pocket. Then the dwarf turn down 40th headin fuh Eighth Avenue.

At Eighth he take out sumfin fum the pocket of his funky long coat, pull it over his face. Birdie who be pretty close behind him see it is a rubber mask of a freaky-lookin whiteman wif a long upsweeping nose an he need a shave. Soon as the dwarf have this mask settled a hooker stop him laughin, she call him Nex or Nix, some shit. The dwarf give her sumfin fum his pocket too. They at 40th and Eighth now. The brothers in front of the movie dealin faro cards know the dwarf too — leas they grin at him like they do — an the dwarf stop to look but not to play. One of the jive brothers grinnin say to Birdie: "Hows by you, Miss Humpty Doo?" Birdie don pay him no mind.

The dwarf walkin east to Broadway but then he turn west again at 44th. Birdie don know what he up to, it sure ain cold, she start to sing. The dwarf turn aroun an look at her, maybe even smile through the mask. Then — they still walkin — he stick his hand in his coat pocket an pull out a long feather. He stick the feather under his mask so he look like a Indian or shit. Then he wave his hand behind his head like he be wavin at Birdie. She jus keep singin and hummin payin him no mind. Fak was she be gettin tired, fo a little dude he din walk all that slow neither. A blind bro wif a meanass dog stop him at the corner of Eighth. Birdie back up quick move acrost the street, she watch the dwarf give him sumfin fum his pocket.

He do this a whole lot, stop an give some beggar sumfin, but fak was din really look like he be givin them money — sumfin else, Birdie din know what. He be walkin stone west fuh the river it seem like, that funky-ass mask an feather all humped an shit — two kids wif some whitelady's purse in their hand come fas round the corner knock the dwarf down run right over him. The dwarf din get mad or nuffin, jus pick hissef up an keep on walkin...

Even before she see it she smell it—the river. It sure smell funky too, Birdie don like it. Then they there an crazy jive down by the river, whole lotta people be crashin an shit, black wif white but all like beggars, small little lights—fires, people cookin, also music, some kinda drums, beggars they come out to meet the dwarf laughin an jivin, callin him Nix like that other done. When the dwarf finish greetin them he like smooth out his feather wif his han, then turn around, say: "How do it feel, Birdie?" He be holdin sumfin in his hand...

quick-like
cold now
Birdie back up fade away fum
the shitass river

Shambling back through the neon long streets to the bus terminal it has begun to sleet, Birdie is cold, she keeps repeating: " 'How do it feel, Birdie?' jive dwarf wan tuh know." By the time she reaches the terminal she is sopping, singing these same words: "How do it feel Birdie / jive dwarf wan tuh know / How do it feel jive..."

SMOKE

SMOKE

Humps of cloud pushing

Humps of cloud pushing east out of Jersey. Cora was looking for Flatbush. It would have to be fall. She was about to take a smoking cure. She inquired of a citizen, who, introducing himself as Duane, said, "I can't say about Flatbush, but there's Canarsie. What's left of it." The man, smiling oddly, was pointing with his gloved fist: where Canarsie had been was rubble, random swirls of white acrid smoke.

somewhere in Flatbush, sitting on the charred wooden steps of the African Methodist Episcopal Zion Church, a man. A ruin of a man.

Zion... A ruin of
a man

Cora stopped at a luncheonette. Her waitress wore an orange and white smock with an American flag lapel which read, PATTI. As she was writing Cora's order a man's deep voice on the intercom said: "Patti, please report to the cage." Patti told Cora, "Excuse me," and left. Cora took a dime from her purse and went to the public phone

cage. Patti

at the rear of the luncheonette. After the second ring his machine came on asking for a message. Cora said, "I want to confirm my appointment for the smoking cure. My name is Cora. The problem is I still haven't found Flatbush.

I still haven't found
Flatbush

derelict? transient? Not a beggar. He asks for nothing. He sits on the steps of the burned-out AME Zion Church asking for nothing.

The phone was next to the lavatories. Cora stepped into the LADIES. Through the grimy window above the basin the day looked drear. She entered the stall, had only begun to pee—when a furious scratching at the door, a shrill loud voice: "Let me in I have to come in! I can't—"

I can't

he wears a tattered greatcoat, black, buttoned to the throat. A blue watch cap pulled down over his ears. He is asking for nothing. His bony legs are crossed at the knees. Eccentric, this posture, for a transient who has nothing, asks for nothing. Look, though, at his eyes.

eyes

It was the voice of a deranged woman. Her ravaged head she actually thrust into the stall. Cora, up off the stool, stepped out: vile moist sinking underfoot notified—*too late*. The woman had voided her bowels on the floor outside the stall and fled. Both of Cora's shoes were filmed with it.

too late . . . voided

Both of Cora's shoes
were filmed with it

the eyes demand NOTHING. Bony long legs, ravaged high-boned face, glaring deep-set eyes. He has stuffed newspaper into the rents in his soles.

rents in his soles

Cora was moving in the direction of Flatbush. At frequent intervals she paused at a curb to scrape her shoes. The matter adhered, she stank of it. Cora thought—pity and nausea—of the moist smoking pile on the chipped tile floor by the basin. It was fall, the keepers of the green were burning leaves despite the ordinance. Cora lit a cigarette, her final (she hoped) one.

The matter adhered

the transient has now moved several feet away from the church, is kneeling, gazing intently at the pavement. Youths are coursing through the street. In tandem, swiftly, their eyes fierce and blank. Male, female, swift and blank— they run over the churchbum, slam him to the pavement.

swift and fierce, blank

"Call me Duane. I used to be Anton. That colored church? Heck, took them twelve years to raise the bucks. They touched every black that had a dime and finally got the damned thing up. A small sort of church but with lots of room for them to sway and sing near the altar. They stuck young cedars in the tiny lawn. This was about a month ago. Two Fridays ago sumbitch burnt down. Insurance investigator said it was the sexton frying

hog fat in the sacristy. The sexton and some of the other Negroes —they claim arson."

Cora was told she had to take the subway. It was Duane, with the smooth black glove on his hand, who smilingly directed her to the narrow entrance in the pavement. On the Local, Cora fumbled in her purse for her book, couldn't find it, remembered she had been reading it in the restaurant lavatory. Must have left it there. In her mind's eye: the pile, the deranged woman...the stench. Her lost book? A paperback volume of Nellie Sachs' verse.

"O the Chimneys"

the prone derelict, chin bloody, one ear to the littered pavement, either has passed out or fallen asleep. He lies asprawl, people pass by.

When Cora asked the woman sitting to her left whether this was the train to Flatbush, the woman shrugged. Cora saw then that she was Hispanic, evidently did not understand English. And yet the tabloid opened on her lap was in English. Cora (not meaning to be uncivil) was compelled by a story at the top of the page and, over the woman's shoulder, read it through. It seemed that a plastic bag fell from a sanitation truck onto a West Side street. The bag split open and aborted fetuses rolled and slid into the street. Other vehicles ran over them or catapulted them onto the

aborted fetuses rolled
and slid

struck a man with an
Armenian name in the
shoulder

she died in the
ambulette

rent in the other sole

sidewalk. One struck a man with an Armenian name in the shoulder, another landed just inside the entrance to a bank. Pedestrians had to sidestep; an old woman, angrily trying to kick one of the viscous things out of the way, slipped and fractured her coccyx. She died in the ambulette on the way to the hospital. The very hopital, as it turned out, in which these embryos and fetuses had been bagged. Or so the article reported.

slowly the derelict collects himself, picks up something from the pavement which he puts into his cap, makes his way back to the church steps. He looks up at the sky, examines his left shoe, feels with a bony rigid hand the rent in his sole. He examines the rent in the other sole. He withdraws the newspaper from the rent in his right sole, uncrumples it, separates a piece and puts it in his mouth. Then he crumples it again and stuffs it into his shoe. These details absorb him. The vapor rises from his nose and mouth.

Cora felt like a cigarette. She had just emerged from underground onto a street which would have to be in Flatbush. It seemed cold for fall. Near the subway exit a man was selling raccoon tails to factory women on their lunch break. A slender young man with a beard and a smooth delivery. While Cora scraped her shoes against the curb

You ax what it cos?

smiled...bought

still haven't found
Flatbush

she listened: "Yawl look what I got. Round yo neck, madam. You too, lil sister. You ax what it cos? Cos you almost nothin and treat you real tenderly. Just seventy-five cent, lil sister, and one of these yere lovely furry things be yours. And a prized accessory to yo wardrobe too, cause you can wear em wif anythin..." Several of the women smiled, some stopped, bought. Cora asked one of them whether she was in Flatbush.

again the derelict has moved away from the AME Zion Church steps—what's left of them. Kneeling, gazing intently at the pavement, occasionally picking something up, putting it in his cap. The sky appears to be changing.

Cora, it seemed, was in Coney. She was told that Flatbush was a bus ride away. Heat curled up from the manholes. She wanted to smoke. She stopped by a phone on the corner, dialed. Again it was his machine. "My name," she said, "is Cora. I'm on my way. For the smoke cure. Only I still haven't found Flatbush."

evidently he has what he needs. He has moved back away from the street to the church steps. What the derelict has collected in his watch cap are bottle caps, and he is proceeding to lay them out on the step in a kind of pattern. Bent and bony, intensely concentrated on assem-

abolitionist

Mass
snow

bling his bottle caps, he resembles a Massachusetts abolitionist minister of the 1840's attending to some detail of the Mass. It has begun to snow.

Duane: "Bedwetters, smokers, a-theists—I handle them all. On the whole women make the best subjects. I've burnished an old Greek cross, hold it steady twelve inches in front, five inches above her eyes. When they close I pass my implement slowly across her trunk: smoking gone, she's mine. Apollinaire was wounded at Verdun and trepanned sixty-five years ago yesterday. My left gloved hand held the surgical saw."

Cora had to walk several blocks to the bus stop. She was cold and tired. Her mind kept switching to the deranged woman in the toilet. Her shrill pleading voice had had in it the tremolo of a child. Cora lit another cigarette. At the junction, workmen on ladders were removing the Christmas lights. Cora's bus (number 88) was there. The driver closed the door as soon as she boarded, held out a gloved hand for her fare.

tremolo of a child

(number 88)

bent

revive union

bent, intensely focused on his bottle caps on the uneven ruin of steps, his face reddened from the cold, he resembles Moctezuma's dreamer (his nation flaming), entranced—futilely—to revive union.

Here's your Flatbush,
Missy

"O the Chimneys"

huddled against

The driver suggested that Cora sit behind him. After fifteen or twenty minutes he turned to her and grinned, pointing with a smooth gloved finger. "Here's your Flatbush, Missy." Cora stepped off the bus into snow! She couldn't believe it. When she had started out it was a mild fall day. Now she was tromping through two, three inches of snow, and it was snowing yet, thickly, over her uncovered head and cotton shawl. She glanced at her watch: twenty before two. She looked for a phone but didn't see one. She ducked under the lee of an off-track betting parlor and opened her address book. Then she remembered: she had written the address of the smoke cure on the flyleaf of her Nellie Sachs, the volume she had left in the toilet. All she recalled of him was his first name: Anton. She lit a cigarette.

his bottle caps assembled, he sits with his gaunt reddened face and black greatcoat, bony legs crossed, deep-set eyes unblinking under the pulled-low watch cap. Workers, shoppers, huddled against the snow, pass by; derelict stares straight ahead, does not follow them with his eyes.

Cora was trudging through the snowy deserted streets of Flatbush. A public phone on the corner: she inserted her dime, dialed. Something was wrong—no dial tone. The phone was broken. It was the last coin she had

last coin she had. Wet and cold, shivering, she continued to walk, not knowing where.

from his spot on the steps the derelict sees the slim young woman trip, fall, struggle to stand, slip to one knee. He is off the steps and to her side, steadying her by elbow and wrist, leading her up the charred wooden steps to the surprising shelter of the burned-out church front. Once there he removes his greatcoat and drapes it across her shoulders. He sits her down on the step across from him on the opposite side of the checkerboard. Half the bottle caps are laid out convex side up, the others, concave side up. After catching her eye he extends a blue bony finger and pushes one of the convex-side-up caps diagonally to the left. Cora stares dreamily at him, then at the checkerboard. Trembling, she extends her thin-wristed hand...

Duane: "It's winter, she'll weary of his bottle caps, his glowering rectitude, the stench of the smoldering church. Or maybe he'll die first. Either way, slime gone, she'll want to stop smoking in earnest. What I mean is her need will seep out of her juices. Which is where I come in. I've got the fingers for it."

SANNTO

(for S.B.)

SANNTO

Sannto gave his elusive mild smile. "This is my second circle of torment," he said, handing Rosen the sheet of paper.

Sannto had not introduced the three young girls who stood uneasily next to him in Rosen's living room. It was 8:20 on a Sunday morning. Sannto's rhythmic tapping at the side door had gotten Rosen out of bed. Initially Rosen had confused the tapping with the drumming of woodpeckers. Two downy woodpeckers, a male and a female, regularly drummed on the pin oak near his bedroom window.

Until this morning Sannto had always made his monthly or bimonthly visit solo. Today he was accompanied by three young girls. In varying degrees all three looked to be part Shinnecock like Sannto. They seemed distinctly uneasy and somewhat bored—

"This is my second circle of torment," Sannto repeated smiling.

"Ah." Rosen nodded. The paper was as usual printed in pencil in a small, painstaking, left-leaning hand without margins, and it filled both sides. The title at the top of the page was "The Second Circle of Torment."

Just then one of the girls giggled—Rosen had no idea at what.

"How about some coffee?" he offered.

Sannto smiled.

"Why don't you all sit down. I've put some water on."

Rosen was in his pajamas and barefoot. He shuffled into the kitchen with Sannto's "poem" in his hand. Sannto's writings looked like prose, but the connections between observations were elliptical, more like poetry. Sannto called them poems. It was the fourth such writing Sannto had presented him with in the year or so they were acquainted (a colleague and Sannto's prime benefactor at the college first asked Rosen's permission, then encouraged Sannto to audit Rosen's weekly

graduate seminar in "Aboriginal Ideologies"). Five or six weeks ago
Sannto had walked into Rosen's class late (this was usual), paused at
his desk and handed him a sheet of paper entitled "The Circle of
Torment." The piece Rosen now held in his hand was evidently an
extension of the earlier one.

Rosen stood near the simmering kettle and rapidly read through
Sannto's poem:

THE SECOND CIRCLE OF TORMENT

As I approached the course of battle water my eye darkened
leaving behind the sea.

The second human spirit becomes fit to send to heaven.

But here let the dead rise again.

I saw in my vision of the unseen that someone was pulling a
rope across the road. Attached to the rope was a rat.

The rat ran under the water that was on the road. When he
came up he had a bubble on his back, sliding his chin on
the ground.

But the rat did not die.

I saw something coming out of the wall. It looked like
a pig with a hard shell on its back. I also saw in a
room where it was full of eyes, two people dancing in a
circle. While the two people were dancing rats were
coming out of the wall. They were covered with green
silk like stockings. The rat jumped up and bit someone
on the neck.

This was discovered around a grave that was second closest
to heaven, some people say they had goat legs on their bodies
and nowhere to use them.

Then I saw a hand at the window wearing a glove with two
fingers showing. One son dropped his book, sliding it
on the ground like the rat sliding his chin on the ground.
One son came to him, opening his mouth so I could look
down his throat. On one side of his mouth I could see
his palate. On the other side I could see a lobster with
glittering eyes making a funny noise as if it was breathing.

I was walking to the top of the mountain and when I got
there I saw lakes of water. I also saw two ladies standing
on the other side calling out to me. One of the ladies
looked familiar to me. This was a time when I was under
the life of the unseen.

As he had expected Rosen recognized several of the images from

Sannto's previous writings. When he returned to the living room with five cups of coffee on a tray, Sannto and the three girls were still standing. The girls appeared more restless than before, shuffling their feet and shifting positions *vis-à-vis* each other. They were pretty girls, all three, and nubile too, though they couldn't be older than fifteen or sixteen. Sannto himself would be in his early or middle forties, though this was hard to know.

Rosen motioned them to have some coffee and they did, each of the girls taking up her cup and saucer a little tentatively. They were standing together abreast, with their backs to the bay window, not precisely in front of the window but angled away from it. The window looked out on a grove of pignut hickory and red cedar. The oblique morning sun played about their supple ankles. They sipped their coffees carefully.

Sannto said: "You have read my poem?"

"I did, yes. In the kitchen. But I'd like to read it again, at my leisure. I can hold on to this for a while?"

Sannto nodded. "I have made seven."

They had gone through this before. Instead of making Xerox copies, Sannto rewrote his poem six times and presented copies to various souls. He used whatever paper he could get. Rosen's copy contained the printed legend, THOMAS L. MULLANEY / CIVIL ENGINEER-ING CONSULTANT / JOB'S LANE, SOUTHAMPTON, centered at the top of the sheet. Sannto had written over this inscription as if it didn't exist.

"I will read," Sannto said, relieving Rosen of his poem.

Now this was unexpected. Sannto had never before volunteered to read one of his writings aloud. The girls meanwhile had altered their position and now stood at a ninety degree angle to the window; they appeared neither to be looking outside nor at anything specific within the room (in fact there were several unusual things to look at in the wide room: textile hangings, Navaho sand paintings, wood and stone artifacts). The girls held the cups and saucers in their hands, arms extended away from their bodies.

Standing stiffly and holding the paper in both hands in front of his face, Sannto read in a rather loud unmodulated tone which seemed to grant each word equal weight. He read without raising his eyes.

Listening, it occurred to Rosen that he did not understand the significance of seven. Sannto appeared always to make—interestingly, he invariably said "make" ("*poiēsis*": Greek), not "write"—seven versions of a particular poem. Four, three, eight—these were the critical numerals for northeast Native Americans. Where did seven fit in?

Primarily, though, Rosen was again awed at the spectre of this uneducated reservation Shinnecock who evidently had never traveled out of New York State coming up with such potent archetypal stuff. Even accepting that Sannto was schizophrenic (Rosen's colleagues insisted on this), there was a visionary coherence about his writings which recalled thought processes endemic not only to North American, but to Asian, African, and Amazonian Basin aboriginals as well.

In theory it was not especially unusual even for elusive inward states to be described similarly by aboriginals separated by geography. Anthropologists called this phenomenon "parallel development." But commonly an investigator had to uncover much earth and rock and waste to come up with even a trace of this "ore." In Sannto's case it was right there, obviously infusing his every day. The "pig with the hard shell on its back," the rat attached to the rope, the "goat legs," the "breathing" lobster "with glittering eyes." These tropes and others too had their origin far, far back in anthrohistory.

As Sannto read the three girls had again shifted their positions and now described a semi-circle, their faces turned entirely to the window. One of them was tapping her feet, evidently impervious to Sannto's "Second Circle of Torment."

When Sannto finished he didn't look up right away, but paused, as if in suspension. Then he smiled and handed the paper back to Rosen. As Rosen glanced at it he could feel Sannto's eyes on him. Outside in a cedar he heard a mockingbird sing.

"Interesting. I think it's a strong piece, Sannto."

Sannto continued to gaze at him expectantly. This was the hardest part of these transactions; Sannto always seemed to want a specific and detailed response to his poems. Yet they were obviously "designed" not to be understood in a literary way, and a psychoanalytic response would of course be inappropriate.

Rosen sipped his coffee. He turned to the window. One of the girls continued to look outside; the other two were facing in. Each still held her now empty cup and saucer at nearly arm's length, as if it were a minuscule bed pan. Rosen smiled at his simile. Likely the girls had never taken coffee in a white bourgeois' living room. Their unease was understandable.

"You can put the cups down on the table," Rosen said.

The girls must not have realized he was addressing them; they didn't respond. Outside the mockingbird continued its elaborate song. It sounded closer. Rosen turned to Sannto.

"Do you hear the mockingbird?" He motioned to the window.

Sannto, smiling, nodded.

"It's a splendid song, isn't it? So full of startling phrases. And yet unlike the robin, for example, one song is rarely the same as the next. Still you can always distinguish that it is that fine singer, the mockingbird. That's the way your poems seem to me, Sannto. This one— 'The Second Circle of Torment'—contains strong images and fine language. It resembles some of your other pieces; at the same time it seems original..."

Even as Rosen was weaving his reply, he could see that it was going to fall short.

When he finished he and Sannto continued looking into each other's eyes for a moment. Sannto's fine-boned Negro-Indian face (there were virtually no unhybridized Shinnecocks left) was taut as always, his black eyes remote and unblinking.

"It is," Sannto said in his uninflected monotone, "my second circle of torment."

There was a pause. Rosen didn't know quite how to take this.

"That's right," he replied weakly. Then he added: "But what is the nature of this torment, Sannto?"

Sannto's countenance didn't waver. Nor did he respond. Rosen turned to the girls. All three now were facing the window. One was rotating her hips rhythmically, as if to music. They still held their coffee cups. Rosen picked up the tray and relieved them of their cups and saucers. He set the tray on a table—then took it up again and went into the kitchen. It was ten past nine. His wife would be getting up soon, and Sunday was Rosen's day to prepare breakfast. He considered inviting Sannto and the girls to stay for breakfast but immediately thought better of it. He shouldn't have asked Sannto what his torment meant. How could he answer such a question? Rosen didn't actually know what he had meant in asking the question. The words had just slipped out. He must have felt uneasy. Sannto's untimely visit and, particularly, the girls—their unexplained presence and peculiar unresponsiveness—made him a little uneasy.

When Rosen, still holding Sannto's poem, returned to the living room Sannto was standing where he had stood, but now the girls were squatting on the floor, two with their backs to the window and the third across at an obtuse angle. Their apparent settling in made Rosen more uneasy than their restlessness. He would try to wind it up.

"Sannto, thanks for coming. I know you'll be dropping in on the class. By then I will have gone through your piece again. Okay?"

Sannto was smiling. "What did you say?"

"What? When?"

"Before."

"Oh. I asked you about the nature of your torment. What I meant—"

"About the mockingbird."

"Oh. Right." Rosen repeated more or less what he had said about the mockingbird.

"I don't hear it now."

Rosen listened. "No. It's stopped singing. It will start again. This is courting season."

For some reason Sannto laughed—either at what Rosen said, or at some private association. Then, while laughing with his mouth open, he opened it wider still and yawned. This was a deliberate, even slow-motioned, gesture, and Rosen was permitted a look first at his teeth, then into his throat. His teeth—Rosen had not noticed this before—were badly discolored, pocked with decay. Four teeth on top, two canines and two bicuspids, were missing.

"Does the mockingbird sing of torment?" Sannto said suddenly.

This utterance took Rosen by surprise. "No, of course not. I didn't mean to diminish—"

Rosen paused in mid-sentence. The girls were making a noise. The two who had been squatting abreast were now facing each other and clapping their hands together in a child's game. They were counting as they clapped.

Rosen listened to the rapid rhythmic clapping until number 18, then said with an attempt at lightheartedness: "You never even introduced your friends, Sannto." He motioned with his head to the girls.

"My cousins," Sannto said.

"They are? All three?"

The girls had stopped clapping. Two were standing; the other with her back to Rosen still squatted, her jeans stretched tightly across her loins.

"We are all cousins on the reservation," Sannto said.

"I see." Rosen knew this wasn't literally true, but he didn't question it. He was hungry. He heard his wife stirring above him.

Out of civility Rosen was about to ask Sannto and his "cousins" to stay for breakfast, when Sannto—as if in anticipation—held up his hand.

"We go."

The third girl was now standing. The three had moved away from the window and formed a circle about Sannto. Their faces were blank.

Rosen's wife meanwhile had come down the stairs.

"Sannto," she smiled. "I didn't know you were here." She noticed the girls of course and glanced at Rosen inquisitively. "Perhaps Sannto and his—"

"Cousins," Rosen said.

"—would care to stay for breakfast."

"We go," Sannto, the familiar smile on his face, said. He was backing up toward the door. The girls moved with him, maintaining the circle. As he was about to pass through the door Sannto offered Rosen his hand. This was his standard procedure. His hand was surprisingly small and as always he applied no pressure and withdrew it at once. The girls left silently and without a glance at either Rosen or his wife.

Mrs. Rosen was naturally curious about what had happened, especially about the three young girls. Rosen, over breakfast, recounted the events as best he could.

THE ARTIFICIAL
SON

THE ARTIFICIAL SON

The Hasid turned left at the corner and Brooklyn died. He stopped. He looked up then down then up again. He looked behind him but there was no behind.

This mask is known as a "spirit-trap." It is human-size and hollow. One slips into it. Scarification marks on either side of the broad nose.

Pinchos the Hasid worked in diamonds on West 47th Street in Manhattan, was due there in less than an hour. The IRT subway which transported him was gone. It had been *here,* just here, around the corner he always turned. Now they would worry—the Hasidim with whom he worked—worry that he was mugged or maybe murdered by a Negro. Pinchos, eighteen, born and bred in Crown Heights, Brooklyn, spoke Yiddish, Hebrew, a little Polish. Now he was stuck.

The scars are in high relief, the eyes are cowry shells, the entire figure is finely carved out of hard wood and it is hollow. It is in a sense a puppet and its function is to lament.

He was walking again, shuffling along beneath his black felt hat, in his long gabardine coat. The pavement had become dirt pocked with stone. The familiar shops selling religious articles, funerary appointments, sect-food were gone. Instead of tenements were cylindrical stones, hills of soil and rough growth, an occasional tree. He was worried. It didn't look like a slum exactly, but it may have been Africa. If so there would be Negroes. His Talmud was in the pocket of his coat, his keys in the pocket of his trousers. He wrapped his fist about his keys: synagogue key, Holy Ark key, apartment keys, diamond center workroom keys. These keys on a steel ring represented his sole defense against the Negroes.

The raffia hair is gathered together under a fez-like head-covering or skullcap. The floor-length robe is fashioned out of coarse cloth, sacking. The most remarkable feature surely is the hands.

He had already traversed the distance of two city blocks since turning the corner, and it still wasn't Brooklyn. The sky was big. He noticed it through the corner of one eye. He had never seen such a thing. It was blue and clear and very broad and it made him uneasy. With his right hand in his trousers gripping his keys, and his left hand in his coat gripping his Talmud, he walked faster. He muttered phrases from the Mishnah. The loose stones pricked the soles of his feet through his worn shoes. He shuffled along rapidly with his gaze down and on a straight course for many minutes and nothing changed. There was not a single person to be seen. Nor were there Negroes. It couldn't be Africa.

The slender hollowed hands are extended palms out in an attitude of imploration. This gesture is distinguished by its grace as by its humility. The extended hands are compassionate and impersonal as the boughs of a tree.

Could it be Israel? Israel was better than Africa but Israel was also tref. Pinchos was sweating. He withdrew his hands from his pockets and loosened his prayer shawl which was draped about his neck and under his coat. He removed his hat and his yarmulke and wiped his sweating head and beard with a handkerchief. He cast a sidelong glance at the sky—it was the same, it was still not Brooklyn. He continued to walk, though less rapidly, with his coat unbuttoned and his heavy broad-brimmed hat pushed back on his head. It was hot. It shouldn't have been hot since it was nearly winter. He was certain of this because winter always coincided with a large shipment of diamonds from Cape Town. And the shipment had come the previous week. Why then was it hot? Again Pinchos looked at the sky, this time with both eyes. He didn't see a sun. Nor were there clouds. Just then a low branch snagged his hat and it fell to the ground. He scarcely noticed. He was pushing uphill, he was tired. Still not a soul. Not even—it occurred to him—a bird. He removed his long black coat and carried it on his arm.

It felt heavy on his arm also. He continued walking for a time, but then he slipped to his knees and rested beneath an overhanging rock.

The native word for this spirit-trap is sometimes rendered as "artificial son." Artificial is not here used invidiously; on the contrary, it implies something like "intercessor" or "surrogate."

When he rose again he had left his coat behind. He trudged ahead. His prayer shawl hung from one shoulder and dragged on the ground. Pinchos wondered what time it was. His wrist watch had stopped and he didn't understand the unchanging sky. He was already late for his job, that was certain. He no longer cared, was too tired to care. Still he continued to labor uphill since it was that or turning back and there was no back. He ripped open the buttons of his shirt to get some air, but soon even this was not enough and he tore off his shirt altogether. The Talmud and his keys he now carried in the pocket of his trousers and the heavy ring of keys was scratching his leg. He transported the keys in his hand for a time, then he let them drop to the ground. Aloud he repeated phrases from the Mishnah and then from the commentary on the Mishnah, the Gemara. It was less the meanings of these ancient texts than the repetition of their sounds which occupied his mind and kept him from appraising his situation. The half-naked Hasid trudged and pushed uphill muttering and sometimes shouting words and phrases from the Talmud. The sunless sky beat down upon him and he didn't know where he was.

If a man dies and leaves no son to mourn him, the artificial son bemoans him. If a creature is afflicted or oppressed or irrevocably alone, the artificial son implores God for him.

At the foot of a stunted cone tree he stumbled onto his knees, and grabbing hold of an exposed root of this tree to keep from rolling downhill, he closed his eyes... When he awoke it was the same, the shiny sunless sky, the heat. He pulled and kicked off his trousers (the Talmud left in one of the pockets) and continued uphill, his striped underwear about his thin shanks, his white socks and black city shoes, the black silk yarmulke on the top of his head, the rest of him beige, naked, vaguely amphibian in the uncanny light. He had not ceased to mutter words from the Talmud, but now these words were punctuated by other sounds, more instinctive: sighs, labored breathing, childlike whimpers.

The artificial son is not white. There is a species of conifer that raggedly grows on the steep hillside. It sends its roots out rather than down into the inhospitable earth. It shelters creatures. Its bole is brown and deeply creased. The artificial son is brown and creased.

He was parched. He pulled a spiny plant out of the earth and squeezed it hard with his hand—he felt moisture and licked his fingers, tasting his own salt blood. He recognized the salt but not the blood. He uprooted another plant from the parched soil, it too was waterless. He did these things as he moved, stumbled uphill, forward. He moaned, he uttered pious phrases, the words and moans indistinguishable in the thin air. He heard, he thought, a child weeping, it came from above and below and every side of him. He didn't pause. His arms and legs were abraded, bleeding, and now there was a different wet—he had emptied his bladder. Without stopping he shook his penis and brought the droplets to his mouth: from every side of him gagging, weeping.

The artificial son is nailed to a tree. Not nailed, depending from a branch. It is darkness.

Pinchos was no longer Pinchos. How could he be? He heard but still did not entirely hear the child. The foothills were mountain, he struggled upward not looking back. Only once did he pause, hearing the thin piercing scream of a bird. He strained his ears, swiveled his head, looked up: nothing. Then he looked down, below, whence he came—it was dark. Again he looked up: the blue-white sky was black, spiked with stars, a moon like a curved sword. And cold. As abruptly as it had become dark, it became cold. The naked boy shivered.

Pinchos is in his eighteenth year, his body wants to live. The sky is studded with light, it lights his way up-mountain, he is moving to fight the cold. It is a fight he will lose quite soon unless he finds shelter.

The artificial son hangs from the branch of a cone tree. A tree ragged and stunted, wind-hurt on the windward side of the mountain, rooted in the poor soil, its roots snaked around rock. In the cold dark the boy on his knees stumbles into this tree, knocks the spirit-trap from its branch, gropes it with his hands, fits it over his head, his body... Standing there now, palms extended, no longer cold; supplicating, fixed, having exchanged grief for *grief*.

GEORGE GROSZ

GEORGE GROSZ

Kristallnacht, Fall, 1938,

Plato was born into a distinguished Athenian family which on his father's side extended back even to the god Poseidon. Philosophy, White-

George Grosz, a resident of the U.S. for the last five years, completes his *Still Life with Walnuts*. About this genre, Grosz, twenty-five years before, declared

head declared, not only derives from Plato, but is in effect a "footnote" to Plato. Except for the provisionally favorable words in his brief "Ion," Plato had little good to say for *poiēsis*. Disorder, insurrection, hubris: these were Art's presumptions.

that in a time of oppression and barbarity, still lifes, cubist guitars, and other examples of so-called pure art were cowardly evasions. The year is 1913, Grosz is twenty years old. In 1915, he is released from the German army (Grenadier Regiment 2, 1st Kompagnie Bezirk-

"Arma amens capio nec sat rationis in armis." "Frenzied,

Kommando) after suffering an emotional collapse. An attendant symptom, according to the examining physician, is the extreme swelling on his forehead. Grosz's own dia-

I take up arms, but judgement lies not in arms." (Virgil) "Judgement" resides of course in breeding. Longinus: "Certain passions are found which are far removed from sublimity and are of a low order, such as

gnosis was that he had been "thinking too much." In any event, released from the inflamed groin of the German military to the diseased bowel of the German polity, Grosz resumes the work. His

pity, grief and fear." Aristotle (who dandled moon-mad Alexander) acknowledged pity, grief and fear, declared that the well-knit tragedy evoked them in order periodically to purge us of them in Aristotle's

style already moving away from derivative Futurism, derivative Dada, to the spare, hollow, mostly pen and ink, satires. "Satire" does scant justice to his frenzied recordings of Hate's pestilence. "All around me is darkness black like bones. My loathing has grown to enormity. It seems I shall slowly approach the madness of despair." The humans

undemotic world. Multiply Antigone's woes ten millionfold, diminish her caste, lend her skin pigment...Aristotle saw simulacra in Sophocles' strophes; Sophocles

in his canvases epitomized by the bubonic signs that govern them. (Among the oddities of modern allopathic medicine

saw. Recall his oddly neglected *Philoctetes:* Apollo's miracle bow and quiver the god had bequeathed to Herakles. When the centaur Nessus' hate and Deianeira's jealousy combined to poison him, Herakles chose Philoctetes to ignite his pyre on Mount Oeta. For this service Philoctetes was rewarded with the miracle bow. Why

is the "bulimia syndrome," wherein the principal experiences a frequent compulsion to vomit. Typically this begins as an occasional dieting "technique" which escapes, so to speak, from cultivation. As one victim put it: "All I seemed to want to do was binge and purge, binge and purge.") Grosz's stunning virulence transfigured his despair only while he worked. Between canvases the hate and nausea lodged

Philoctetes? Why not one of the renowned warriors: Agamemnon, Diomedes, Ajax Telemon? Son of Zeus, Herakles was himself the supreme warrior—who yet knew keen, persistent sorrow. His final "labor" had been to descend to Hades and abduct Cerberus. When, after long years, he emerged, his wife, father and father-in-law, King Creon, had all

—Hindenburg's iron cross—in the throat. In 1918, Grosz joins the Communist Party, and though he soon concludes that Communism *as practiced* is at best a rung above German Fascism, his membership, even more than his canvases, makes him a marked man. 1921: tried and fined for slander; 1923: his ECCE HOMO declared obscene and confiscated by the authorities; 1928: put on trial for blasphemy; 1930: tried once again for blasphemy...Persecution could not contain

been murdered. Next, then, to the Titan Prometheus, Herakles was the great endurer. Philoctetes,

armed with godly bow and quiver, set out against Troy with Odysseus and the kingly sons of Atreus. En route they stopped at the island of Chryse to sacrifice to the local deity. Philoctetes, freshly enobled, kneeled first at the shrine—and was bitten in the foot by a snake. At once, most strangely, the wound inflamed and soon began to suppurate with the vilest stench. Philoctetes had commenced to groan so uncontrollably that they could not continue with the homage. At Odysseus' instigation, the infected warrior (and his bow) were removed to the uninhabited island of Lemnos, abandoned there. Philoctetes

the infection. Woodcuts, pen and ink, watercolors, oils; beginning with the pre-war, proceeding into the so-called Interregnum when the "White Terror" fascists assassinate strikers and young Adolph is aspiring to become an architect, fated homeopath Grosz evacuates into the bowel of our imaginings.

remained there alone for ten years, his noisome wound rendering him almost an invalid. But in the final year of the occupation of Troy, after Achilles and Ajax had been killed and their long enterprise was seeming bleak, the Greeks

Not at work Grosz is a bourgeois: punctilious, finicky, disapproving of "bohemians," of the opinion that revolution is simply and always an "orbital motion about a fixed point, which is power." Inflamed, at work, Grosz is Plato's poet as lightning rod—the primal lunatic energy distilled through him to the ground of his canvas, powering it: *The Pimps of Death; Riot of the Insane; Sanatorium; Germany, A Winter's Tale; Got Mit Uns; Blood is the Best*

abducted the Trojan's soothsayer who confided at last that Troy would fall only if Neoptelemus, son of Achilles, was fighting in his father's armor, and if Philoctetes with his miracle bow was persuaded to join the war. Hence wily Odysseus, accompanied by young Neoptelemus, dispatched to Lemnos to enlist Philoctetes however he can. Aeschylus and Euripides also treated this legend, only their themes had to do principally with the conflict between pride and sacrifice for the common good. Sophocles alone interested himself in Philoctetes' long grievance, kept acute by his stink and pain.

Sauce; White Slaver; Parasites; In Memory of Rosa Luxemburg; The Absolute Monarchist; Munke Punke Dionysius; For the Fatherland—to the Slaughterhouse; Eclipse of the Poor; Hindenburg: 'As I Understand The Republic; Any Monarchist Can Support It With A Good Conscience'...

As with Electra and Antigone, Philoctetes' extreme emotional state possessed not only power but a peculiar dignity which resembled grace. Among artists, this "grace," where it exists, is in the work. I think of Blake, Dostoyevsky, Baudelaire, Van Gogh ...and of Grosz. Because of the special circumstances which acted upon his sensibility, Grosz is preeminently among them.

In Sophocles' scheme it is the idealism and rectitude of young Neoptelemus that neutralizes Odysseus' cold expedience and persuades Philoctetes to let go of his hate and rejoin his comrades in the larger cause. Herakles himself—as *deus ex machina* and as an emblem of Philoctetes' conscience—appears to bless the undertaking. Thus Philoctetes abandons his island, is cured of his wound by the son of Asklepios, and is crucial in the Greeks' ultimate victory in Troy. And yet this noble warrior and public man, in relinquishing his keen bitterness and long isolation, has sacrificed not only that negative, pride, but the alchemical grief borne out of it.

Grosz's "clock stopped in 1932." By the time the Nazis had seized power Grosz and his family were settled in the U.S., and the artist, in his fortieth year, had withdrawn from social commitment. Insisting now that "the working class was the basest of all," and that human-kind was irredeemable, Grosz announced that his new intention was to grow rich in America. To this end he commenced to paint nudes and still lifes and (without tendentiousness) people. To his comrades still in Germany who implored him to convey the Nazi pestilence, Grosz responded by citing the incorruptibility of art and his new consecration. Only, as Edmund Wilson commented, "the colors that Grosz applied to his street scenes were always overflowing their outlines and the Americans he would have liked to idealize turned out to be 'mostly middle-aged and uglier than I had intended.'"

Grosz's stain had pursued him. In the middle 1940's, a jagged hole began to find its way into his canvases, sometimes at the physical center, other times at a periphery. Grosz was by this time a species of public man and quasi-celebrated artist. He was awarded grants and gold medals; was investigated by the FBI, whom he convinced that he was merely another apolitical painter—his youthful depredations in a European country excepted; he was exhibited. There was nothing for it: the infection flared, the hole re-emerged, his line frequently appeared uncontrolled, even deranged. He refused Brecht's request to work conjointly.

In 1959, he returned to Germany for a visit. A month or so later, in Berlin, coming home alone from an evening out, he fell down into the cellar in the unfamiliar house where he was staying, and died. The hole again—it had made its final claim. Tympani, jew's harp, beer-hall accordion...

Wishing Grosz had not turned his back is not to devalue his extended early confrontation. I am chastened by the words of another, whose gift resembled Grosz's, who seemed better adjusted to the Agony; Brecht:

> TO THOSE BORN AFTER
>
> Hatred of baseness, too,
> Distorts one's features,
> Wrath against wrong, too,
> Makes one's voice hoarse. Alas,
> Though we wished to prepare the ground
>   for friendliness,
> We ourselves could not be friendly.

But you when the time has come
For man to be a helper to man,
Remember us
With consideration.

OLD MAN /
BAG-LADY

OLD MAN / BAG-LADY

OLD MAN

Raining. Not raining. The ocean slaps the shore. The spire on the gothic revival church strains upward to...dissolution. This fragment is dedicated to you.

With the index finger of his left hand Lionel Bent spins his globe. It is the upper East Side of New York City. An arthritic old man is pushing his wheelchair through traffic. Onerously, almost mechanically, pushing. Cars, trucks, busses, taxis, limos do not stop. The wheelchair is empty.

The familiar image chafes. Again, reluctantly, Bent spins his globe. (In accord with "fact," its axis is tilted 23.4 degrees, yet there is but a single season.) It is downtown Philadelphia: the old man is pushing the empty wheelchair through traffic, around the occasional pothole, around the gummy smiles of citizens. Bent, feeling the old tug, and wearing merely his skin, fits on the mask the Iroquois call "Old Broken Nose." He shakes his turtle shell rattle then sucks all of downtown Philadelphia through his broken nose, pulverizes it with his mollusk teeth, and expels it in the form of hot ash. It rains over the old man, obliterates him.

Unearthed, the wheelchair is impersonal, fossil, an artifact. Yet for Bent the impression of the near corpse is still traced on the chair. And when he bends to smell the seat the decaying seductive odor is still there. Nor is the old man dead. As in the subsequent frame of a cinema cartoon all is intact once again. Brittle, old, he pushes...And Bent is stuck.

Bent spins: it is perhaps Milwaukee. He has put on the hat of the Kwakiutl, the "wildman," with his white cedar eye and opercule teeth. The hat, though, is small, much too small for his teeming head. By the time Lionel Bent completes the Kwakiutl blessing for old bones, the clan hat has toppled from his head beneath the wheels of a coursing Mercedes.

(Laughter: derisive, but tempered with awe.)

Bent spins: it is the San Francisco "Tenderloin." Buicks, busses... The frail old man is pushing his wheelchair through the ragged thoroughfare. He moves haltingly against the grain of the traffic. He is bollixing it all up. A biker calls him "vermin." Nobody sees him. An occasional child sees him, confusing him with a spiky bush, a bony dog.

Bent compelled to see. Out of the eyeless Cayuga mask, plaited from corn husks and uncured tobacco grown on the graves of medicine men, Bent sees. He sets a match to the "sacrifice bags" of tobacco which compose his forehead. The flames leap to the thoroughfares, the structures, citizens. What follows is accelerated: a Buick with hooks for wheels, spray-painted the color of golden corn in the waning sun and tradenamed "Phoenix," rises like a silicone erection from the teeth of the good, dead citizens. It proceeds to thrust its inflamed member into every orifice, sparing none. It has enormous zest. Among the spawn is the old man, pushing his wheelchair, himself not in it.

The ocean slaps the shore. The oceans strokes the shore. Bent unmasked? An acquaintance described him this way: "Though I know he has never worn glasses, his nose looks somehow raw, his eyes myopic, as if he occupies a strange and blurry place."

Lionel Bent's legs are pale. Nonetheless he fits them into the Zuni breechclout embroidered with trees, a single tree: the immemorial bristlecone pine. Then he forces his large head into a Seneca Long-Nose mask, cloth. In this spirit of ecumenicism he intones ancient words of amity...It appears that the old man's hearing device is inoperative. The citizens wear their tympana on their genitals, they won't hear. Bent has commenced to fast.

After the Ashanti craftsman struck the first blow with his axe, he swallowed some of the sap of the tree, thus declaring his kinship with the tree. When the tree was cut it was left on the ground so that the spirit would find a home elsewhere. History is not history. Africa is spent.

Geneva then: banks. Passion-cubes, ozone, executive cant, petrol. And beneath this dome the old man pushes his empty wheelchair, pushing east to Iran, Pakistan, beggarly India. Here the starving see the hunger in Bent's old man without seeing him. Minarets, bartizans. The muezzins intercept him, pull down his trousers, evaluate his circumcision. Saddhus sprinkle their bodies with the ash of their dead relatives. Bent spins his tilted globe. He rubs his eyes with his fists then focuses again on the old man. He forces on the face of the swerving taxi driver in Singapore. But no sooner is the loutish blindered head set right then it disintegrates, leaving just Bent.

Why is it that the old man's features remain unclear? His knobby skull is bowed, his body of course bowed. Bent, who has conceived him, can't apprehend him. Others gaze at him blankly. Bent spins...He is always on the move. Necessary for him to be so. Not remedial, necessary. But where is his anchorage? The Iroquois say that when a juniper berry drops in the woods, the rabbit will hear it, the hawk will see it fall, the coon will smell it. Bent

Is called obsessive. He is accused of "spilt religion." Birdmasks, horseshoecrabs, spruce. The old man pushes his empty wheelchair through traffic into what remains of forest. The fasting Bent in tow. Toward where "peace is wedded to silence."

Redwinged blackbirds are feeding. Bluejays cawing raucously and feeding, defending their nests. The loggerhead shrike has impaled his vole on a sitka spruce. Bent will not feed until the old man finds his space-

Time. When Bent next stoops to smell the chair he smells almost nothing. Remote smell of very old wood. Biodegradable. The ocean slaps. With the forefinger of his left hand Bent spins his globe. With his other hand he tears his shirt from his body and fastens the Bambara pectoral to his right breast. It is made of old mahogany and cowry shells and represents a hyena. Still spinning Bent's hyena devours the left brain of every human in traffic. Infused then with vegetable, dream, the right brain will

Metamorphose, become

The "reasoning" left. Bent slapping his forehead with the heel of his hand knows this. He's a beggar and a sentimentalist and he can't stop whirling,

And he dedicates his obsession to you.

BAG-LADY

Bent has abducted six citizens from an industrial structure, waylaid them onto the pocked narrowing trail which winds up then down then up, ceasing at the mythopoeic hearth. Crosslegged now on the clay floor, next his hearth, opposite his six, Bent croons:

"That beggar you saw today at noon squatting on her haunches behind her parcels, near the entrance to your building, licking her hands, do you remember?

"Unclothe now, void, remove your jewels. Those are ponchos piled one on the other, they smell of smoke, take one. Form a circle. Close your eyes. Gaze at me in the fireglow. Your noon was fluorescent, not cold, not heat. It is night now, cold swelling moon."

The abducted naked six, Bent intones the names: "Neuresthenic fashion consultant. Senior executive in media relations. Goateed pipefitter. Vice president in charge of accounts. Systems analyst. Master buyer for a 'distinguished' department chain. Close your eyes, remember:

"Your bag-lady squats outside the grey tall building, windowless. Within, the sightless strive, neither seeing the sun nor the bag-lady licking her hands, gazing through pitted eyes (unless her eyes are

"licking her hands" derived from Graham Greene who made a papal fudge of it

closed and her skin is marked). She squats behind her parcels, bags of several dimensions crudely fastened with twine, cartons...

"Lunch called 'Luncheon' within the oblong building. At the appointed time you stride on saurian legs out into the fluorescent light past the bag-lady into the 'Jackal's Palate,' an eating establishment. Here you appraise each other with your eyes and eat and drink with a fierce remoteness. Your post-prandial belches are pistol shots property owners fire at thieves...Your 'property' restored, you re-enter the grey long building with your purpose revived;

"But now the long day is over at last and it's time to wind down time to wind down time to wind down time

"Keep still. Feel the floor. Locate your stomachs. Maintain the circle. Gaze into the fire. Think now. What does the bag-lady keep in her parcels? From your stomach, think now."

their lengthy detour,
their peculiar fear,
have made them weary,
not unreceptive to
Bent's caroling

Lumpish beneath their ponchos, rankless, the goateed pipefitter crawls reluctantly forward, but then stops (Bent croons him over the edge). Several of the bag-lady's parcels display emblems just visible beneath the grime. The goateed pipefitter selects the shopping bag with the most elaborate emblem. Inserting his dexterous flipper-like

"i am the ripe shard

hand into the bag he withdraws himself, child of an absconded plumber, repeatedly abandoned two, three days at a time by his top-ing mama. Grasping his leashed and whining bitch (called Queenie) he whines: "I won't let you go un-less you love me."

The bag-lady's eyes are closed, she sleeps soundlessly.

Bent at his hearth nods his head, coughs, motions the pipefitter to his place in the circle. It is now the mas-ter buyer for a 'distinguished' department chain who (beneath his smoky blanket) sidles forward, thrusts his smooth thick hand into one of the bags and withdraws him-self, age six, his parents in a nasty road accident, his small hand clasp-ing the grey physician's surplice, alarmed child's eyes gazing up at the neutral face, pleading without sound.

The bag-lady's eyes are closed, she sleeps without sound.

The neuresthenic fashion consult-ant's bony hand unringed appears bloodless in the firelight. Un-clothed, she must yet remove her skin's skin before recalling Malaya, touring with three associates, the brown leper had a bell, when he pulled her to him with his eroded hands, groaning in his lunatic tongue: "I won't let thee go except thou bless me."

the world is the gaping anus"

bent: "swallow your then eyes, buyer, swallow"

*The bag-lady produces a sound
from deep within her throat.*

the nethermost
breath: whence the
wound/the song

The tallest lump, the systems
analyst, separates himself, wants to
stand (Bent won't permit him),
instead wriggles to the bag-lady
with a bizarre attempt at decorum,
and inserts three pale fingers into
her bodice. Withdraws them at
once. Inserts them into her least
soiled parcel—but comes up empty.
Unsettled, he thrusts his fingers in
this one or that aimlessly...
emerges with nothing.

*The bag-lady alters her position,
presents him her left side.*

This time the systems analyst makes
contact, withdraws of course himself, a sallow adolescent reading
(for some school assignment) a
microfilmed account of a Con-
golese child, a girl, who had taken
refuge beneath—amazingly—the
udders of a cow and witnessed her
parents and brothers slaughtered
by the Belgian soldiers such rage
such unexpected pity he felt for the
child wishing to hold comfort her
brotherly: "I won't lee thee go
except He blesseth thee!"

Bent's throat is wrinkled, he sings
softly to his bag-lady, carols softly
to his bag-lady:

*The bag-lady's eyes again closed,
she sleeps soundlessly.*

Awake, asleep, the vice president in charge of accounts is without memory. In front of Bent's hearth, facing the bag-lady, this lump can only recite the facts of his transparent personal history. At another (younger) time Bent would have crooned and coaxed. Now he slips the historical dagger with its worn-smooth haft into the rough hands of the pipe-fitter—

bent runs the blade
through his thin
dry hair then moistens
it with his mouth

The bag-lady bears witness to the assassination with closed eyes.

The senior executive in media relations is insensate, which in his instance is an improvement, since he at least has a vegetable awareness of Bent's procedures and even shudders a little when the pipefitter punctures the chest of the accounts-soul...Broadchested (but pigeon-toed), grey "gunfighter's eyes" unfocused, the senior executive in media relations now before the bag-lady: his routinized fingers appraise a parcel as if he were undoing a TV starlet's bra—Bent has the lump withdraw himself at age eight, having (despite his parent's resistance) to identify a playmate electrocuted near the railway trestle, charred bone and teeth...Prospective media-big could not stop dreaming of it, became Roman Catholic at Brown, confessed finally that he (with a child's rage) had pushed the other who then toppled onto the high-voltage wires:

"Father, Father, except thou vent me I won't stop dreaming."

The bag-lady appears to smile, it has nothing to do with the shriven media executive, she sleeps now without sound.

Soon incubus Bent will awake his plantigrades who dream without memory into plantigrades who dimly remember. But now, moving creakily, he feeds the hearth, humming the single tune he knows, it is to his bag-lady.

all we can tell you
of lionel bent is
that he was reared
in texarkana where
he evidently grew
old early

UNDERBELLY
(I)

(for E.H.)

UNDERBELLY (1)

YOGI CLAIMS IMMOBILE RECORD

Kandy, Sri Lanka, July 11 (Reuters)—D.B. Hanumanswami, who was born with a deformed right foot, balanced on his left foot for 28 hours and 48 minutes to claim a world record for standing on one leg. The previous record was said to be 23 hours and 16 minutes.

The 44 year old bachelor yogi, five feet tall and weighing eight stone, was viewed by a large crowd at a bazaar in downtown Kandy yesterday and today. He sang in four languages to pass the time.

Among the languages in which the yogi sang was Malayalam; precisely what he sang in this Dravidian offshoot of Sanskrit could not be translated in a family newspaper, even if it were understood. Sir Hugh Cloaca-Maximus Rosen understood. Sir Hugh, peripatetic editor of the *Guiness Book of World Records,* happened to be trekking for oddities in Southeast Asia when he got wind of Hanumanswami. He flew at once out of Bangkok, engaged a rickshaw at the Kandy aerodrome, and arrived in the bazaar only minutes before the feat was completed.

When it was over Sir Hugh congratulated the diminutive Hindu, then put it to him:

"I say, did you mean what you sang? In Malayalam, I mean."

The Hindu opened his velvet eyes and gazed up at the distinguished questioner with surprise. Yes, of course he meant what he sang.

"I am prepared, you see, to grant you a reward commensurate with your record. Are you at liberty to fly to the U.S.? To New York?"

The fellow appeared not to understand.

Sir Hugh, who had been speaking in Malayalam, repeated his question in Tamil.

This time the yogi understood. Yes, yes, he was at liberty to go anywhere.

"Lovely. I shall work out the arrangements straightaway."

Whence Sri Hanumanswami in grey plaid cap and starched white dhoti appeared at UNDERBELLY ("The Adult Entertainment Center") approximately six weeks later with visa and billfold and a new crutch which resembled a gentleman's walking stick. It was a monsoon Monday morning at seven-fifteen. All was dark both within and without UNDERBELLY. Nor was there any response when the yogi rapped on the large glass doors with his stick.

Sheltering himself beneath the awning Hanumanswami removed his plaid cap and his sandal and waited. Raising his twisted right foot, fitting it into the socket between his left thigh and hip, and extending his arms above his head in an inverted V, Sri Hanumanswami waited silently with his eyes closed. After a time he commenced to hum and then to sing in four languages, Tamil, Malayalam, Sinhalese, and English. He slid from one language to another and back again without conscious design. The effect of the singing was, to American ears, like lamentation; and together with the Hindu's appearance and queer posture it inspired the frantic but open-hearted New Yorkers scurrying to their jobs to drop coins in or near the fellow's cap. The yogi, misconstruing this gesture, assumed that these Americans were acknowledging his world record, even as Sir Hugh had.

At one point, after a few hours of this, Hanumanswami opened his eyes, set down his foot, hobbled to the entrance and rapped again at the glass doors. Still no response. When the Hindu returned to his place he discovered that his cap with the coins in it were gone. Meanwhile other people, men mostly, with complexions dark as his own, and darker, had taken up positions close to his and were extending their own caps. Some were singing, or attempting to sing, in a language which resembled English. He inquired of one of these men about his cap, but the fellow did not respond.

Because of the sudden accumulation of beggars beneath the awning, Hanumanswami was compelled to resume waiting outside in the rain. This he did in his accustomed way, eyes closed, foot tucked, arms together above his head. It was now (the Hindu counted the chimes from a large clock somewhere above) ten o'clock. UNDERBELLY was yet unopen.

The yogi sang, the people streaming by under their umbrellas dropped coins by his foot, while ignoring the other half-dozen or so begging beneath the awning. For his part, the yogi had become so engrossed in his singing that he had entirely forgotten about UNDER-BELLY. But then someone was shaking him by the shoulder.

"Excuse me, brother. Yawl waitin on UNDERBELLY?"

The Hindu opened his eyes.

"UNDERBELLY, bro? Nekkid girls 'n shit?"

"UNDERBELLY?" the Hindu repeated.

"Thas right. I think it open now. Go haid, try the door."

Hanumanswami remembered. He withdrew his foot from his hip, picked up his stick and hobbled over to the glass entrance. So far as he could tell (he wasn't tall enough to have a clear view) it was still dark within. He rapped at the doors. There was no response. Again. No response. When the yogi returned to his place all the coins that had piled up by his foot were gone. He scarcely noticed. Again he raised his twisted foot, closed his eyes, and settled into his singing position. By this time it was high noon, the rain had stopped, and the streets were teeming with workers on their lunch-break. They passed the dark-skinned, barefoot little man in his white skirt making a sweet-sounding lamentation while he stood in his queer posture. They smiled, or shook their heads, or paused to watch and smile and shake their heads, and many of those who stopped dropped coins.

Though Hanumanswami, lost in song, was largely insensible to the curiosity he aroused, one of the other "beggars," the same in fact who had spoken to him before, took it upon himself to act as the Hindu's spokesman.

"Yeah, the brother jus come here...Right, Africa...Thank you for your donation, sister...Thas right, holy. He that alright. Thank you for your donation, bro...No, he always that way, barefoot 'n shit. It the style where he come from...God bless you, bro..."

At two p.m. the lunch recess was over and the passers-by and onlookers had thinned out. Six or eight fellow beggars still encompassed the yogi, including his "spokesman," who called himself Rosen, and claimed to be an Ethiopian Jew descended from the biblical David.

Rosen shook the yogi's shoulder. "How bout some chow, brother?"

The yogi, who was still singing softly, stopped.

Rosen mimed with his hands and mouth. "Chow. Food. Yawl hungry?"

The yogi recalled where he was. In truth he had not dined since boarding the plane in Sri Lanka more than twenty-four hours earlier.

"You hungry, bro? I know a damn good place. Cheap too."

The Hindu waggled his head. This meant yes, he was hungry.

The Ethiopian Jew took his arm. "Hey, yawl wet. An where your shoes at?"

"Shoes?"

"Yeah. Look like some mother copped your shoes. I don't want yawl get sick on us, bro. You a valable property."

"Hey, Ro, I don't think he had no shoes. Dint see none on'm.

Another beggar said this. The Ethiopian turned to him. "Maybe you're right. Hell, les get movin. I'm hungry mysef."

Rosen led the tiny Hindu by his arm, seven or eight of the entourage following. They all ate at a cafeteria and still had enough money left for another meal. At five o'clock Rosen led the yogi back to UNDER-BELLY (which still had not opened), where he sang for the home-coming workers and accumulated at least as many coins as earlier.

That night Rosen found the Hindu a bed, and the following morning he took him to another spot farther east, closer to Fifth Avenue. Here the Hindu assumed his customary position and sang softly in four languages. Rosen and the others squatted or stood around the yogi with their caps and hands outstretched. But as on the day before, it didn't do any good: the white-collar workers and shoppers and occasional strollers didn't notice them, or ignored them, even as they responded to the yogi with smiles and headshakes and money. The day before, in Times Square, it had been mostly dimes and nickels. Today, near Fifth Avenue, it was usually quarters.

Sometimes a passer-by would voice a question, such as, "What the heck is he doing?" or, "Why's his foot stuck in his hip like that?"

This would be the Ethiopian's cue to step forward and explain in his best manner: "I'm glad you ax, brother. He be prain. That the way they do it where he come from. Africa. He come here to tell yawl there be a lot of folks that need..."

Once, as Rosen was gathering up the Hindu's alms and depositing them into a coffee tin he carried for that purpose, an office-worker addressed him indignantly:

"Hold on there, fella! What are you doing with that cripple's money?"

Rosen looked up at his questioner with benign eyes.

"Thank you fuh enquirin, brother. I'm holdin it fuh him. Kinda like a bank do. You see, he come from a very poor family over there in Africa. But wif us he feel real at home since we his brothers and sisters, and besides we jus as poor as him. I'm sure you already knows that. It a goshdarn shame too..."

Rosen and his beggars and the yogi broke for lunch at two-fifteen. Afterwards Rosen bought the yogi a sandal for his good foot at an army and navy store. They returned to their spot just west of Fifth Avenue at four-thirty to catch the white-collars leaving work.

The next day they came back to this location but did not do well. The following morning, then, Rosen led the yogi to another spot, a concrete park between two very tall buildings, one belonging to an oil company, the other to the company's "affiliate." This was one block east of Fifth, at Madison Rosen arranged a small rug on the pavement in the center of the park, then withdrew with the other beggars and lurked nearby trying not to look conspicuous. The yogi removed his shoe, laid down his crutch, took his place on the rug. He did these things slowly, but purposefully, since the spirit of song was strong in him.

People arrived later to work on Madison Avenue, at ten and ten-thirty and even eleven o'clock. And oftentimes they stepped directly from their cars or limousines into the building. Lunchtime was better: some of the lower-echelon workers congregated in the park with their sandwiches, they saw and heard and shook their heads over the yogi, and several dropped their coins. Just before five o'clock the canny descendant of King David lifted the Hindu's blanket with the Hindu still on it and set it between the waiting limousines and the high steel doors of the affiliate building. But when the executives emerged with their pointed noses and slim leather cases they strided past the Hindu and entered their smooth machines without having paused, evidently without having *seen* the crippled beggar.

Rosen, witnessing, shook his head. "Damn! Wunt you know it!"

The following morning they moved farther east to Lexington, setting up between a bank and a "copying center." But here they ran into a difficulty: a palsied family selling pencils, and a broad-shouldered blind man scraping ice which he flavored with syrups, were already dividing the lucrative space. Unwelcome, the Ethiopian and his party moved still farther east to Third Avenue. They set up in front of another bank, it was twenty minutes in front of noon, and Rosen was anticipating a hearty reception—when they were approached by a cop on a horse.

Bending sideways from his saddle he jabbed Rosen in the head with his leather boot.

"What can I do fuh ya, officer?"

The Ethiopian asked the question for civility's sake. He already knew what he could do.

Expressionless, the horse-cop rubbed the thumb and forefinger of his black gloved hand.

"I unnerstand, officer. An how much yawl be wantin?"

The horse-cop responded in a voice an octave or so higher than the Ethiopian would have expected.

"How much? Enough to feed my animal, black guy. You've got eyes. This ain't no fucking crow I'm straddling."

"Uh huh…"

That was Third Avenue. The yogi did what he did. Rosen and his people skipped lunch. At six o'clock the horseman returned and took his cut, two ten dollar bills, which he fitted up his black leather sleeve. That night the beggars slept near the river. Very little to eat, but Rosen played his accordion, one of the others twanged a jew's harp, the yogi sang.

The next morning they returned to the same spot, but it was no good. People had grown used to them. At lunchtime, then, they moved one street farther east, setting up in front of an animal shelter. As the yogi sang the caged dogs and cats and parakeets and cockatiels and hamsters and gerbils keened and howled in accompaniment. Shortly a functionary emerged from the animal shelter. Standing in the glass doorway he shouted to the yogi:

"Cut out the noise! You're exciting the animals."

Rosen stepped forward. "What you signifyin?"

The functionary gave him a sour glare. "I said your noise is exciting the animals."

"Uh huh. And what's wrong wif excitement, bro? Animals got to let it out like anyone else—"

"If you don't leave right now I'll phone the police."

"Gaw haid, rube. Do it. We have our rights."

The animal chorus resumed. Passers-by were amused. They giggled and dropped coins near the yogi's foot. In a brief time a small crowd had accumulated. A woman with a child said:

"I see this one"—she meant the yogi. "But where are the other sounds coming from?"

"From in there, Missus," Rosen pointed. "A whole lotta animals be caged up right in there."

"Is that so?"

"Mommy," her child whined. "I wanna animal. I wanna… mouse."

"Not now, dear."

The woman dragged her child away. But others, with or without children, entered the animal shelter with expressions of discovery on their faces.

Rosen's people had begun to exchange grins and slap each other's palms—when they heard the loud whinny of a large horse. The horse-cop with the countertenor voice had stolen inside their circle. The helmeted head, tilted slightly, was smirking.

"Now ain that a drag!" Rosen said (to himself). To the horse-cop who was rubbing his gloved thumb and forefinger, he said: "I guess yawl wan enough to feed yo animal."

"Not this time, black guy. Your presence here is a violation. Get your broken-hearted asses out of here right now!"

Rosen didn't argue. He gathered up the yogi and led his band to First Avenue. That was about as far east as they could go, short of jumping in the river. While they were dragging east the yogi sang, someone played the jew's harp, another beat upon a small drum. There were maybe fifteen in Rosen's band and they had a dirty-ass look about them too: bony blacks in tattered clothes with long limbs and nasty bulges in their trousers; leprous old women with grimy cluttered shopping bags; an acromegalic Chinese girl of sixteen who towered over the others; a handful of loonies of indeterminate age and race...

As they moved the sky darkened, the pavement gave way to dirt and grass and stone. A foghorn sent its plangent syllable into the estranged air.

The yogi, transported on a "palanquin" made up of hands, sat with his foot tucked, eyes closed, and his face composed into an idiot's calm, his lips mimicking song.

At First Avenue they were compelled to move laterally for several hundred meters, since whatever space they chose was patrolled by fierce dogs or prohibited by signs. It had become cold, on every side tubular stone chimneys belched white smoke. After a considerable time Rosen discovered what appeared to be a congenial spot: an astronomer's tower tapering high into the smoggy atmosphere. Here it was they set up camp, the women preparing to go to the river for water, the men to erect shelter, the yogi of course in their center.

Only minutes after they had stopped, one of their band, a naked angular man with spiny hair, ran shrieking into the street. Immediately came the report of automatic fire—the man fell like a leaf. The gunfire had come from above. Looking up, Rosen saw that the astronomer's tower was actually a rotating stone turret, and circling clockwise high above them were three helmets with powerful guns. One of the helmets was shouting down through a bullhorn:

"Keep moving, vomit! We don't want to waste ammo on your shit-stained hides. But we will if you don't get the fuck out of sight quick!"

He made his point. Rosen's band began to gather up what they had just laid out—when again the report of automatic fire: the giant Chinese girl toppled slowly like an oak.

The bullhorn: "Vomit! Freak ass out of here! Now!"

They did this. Rosen slipped his neck between the yogi's shanks and led his band hastily toward the river. It was night now, but the sky was infused with the white fire from the smokestacks and with the lights from the skyscrapers. The combined glare was sharp enough for Rosen's beggars to see as they made their way.

They heard a peal of bells, a carillon, and fifty meters farther they passed a carousel. Children with luminous skin and fetching smiles straddled their play-animals. They whooped and shrieked with hilarity, kicking with their heels at the horses' sides. The carousel itself was wreathed in grey-white smoke, the smells of candied apples and hot dogs mingling with the thick scent of incense. The band soon saw that quite close to the carousel in the direction of the river was a tottering wooden structure behind a white stone wall; the wall was topped with shards of broken glass. The structure was a leprosarium. Ulcerous faces with vague woebegone eyes pressed against the windows in the wavering light. The burning incense evidently was intended to obscure the stench of infection.

The yogi must have recognized the stench. Astride Rosen's shoulders, he paused in his singing to inquire: "We are where?"

Rosen chortled sardonically. "It ain Africa, brother. If that what you thinkin. This yere's a fatter place, a fuller fuckin gizzard, if you unnerstan what I'm sayin."

The yogi didn't respond for a moment. Then he resumed his singing...

"Hang on tight now, yogi."

They were passing over a cambered bridge. A blind black man in a kiosk tried to sell Rosen a newspaper.

"No way, bro. My newspaper eyes is dead. I'm kinda like the way you is now."

Though the other side of the bridge was quite close to the river, the terrain was hilly and even sere. Only two buildings were visible, the first some fifty meters in front of them. Another atop a rise in the distance. From the look of it Rosen suspected that the closer structure was a bank or lending house. But then they heard the desperate plaintive lowing of cattle punctuated by the heavy chonk of cleaver on wood. An abattoir—they could smell it.

The other structure had to be a church. For one thing it was Sunday and even from where they were Rosen could make out the tidy pink-skinned twosomes holding each other's arms, milling about. Clearly it was no ordinary church: it had a sort of steeple, circular tiers, and what looked like elaborate carvings on the stone exterior.

"It's a pagoda, boss."

Someone had spoken these words in Rosen's ear. It was the yogi.

Rosen nodded. "I guess that's what it is alright."

The beggars soon saw that this church or "pagoda" wasn't for just any soul. Menacing Doberman pinschers paced furiously on the lowest tiers. And signs stuck in the ground proclaimed in various languages that the church was RESTRICTED.

Rosen stopped. He held up his hand and his people also stopped.

He said to them: "Yawl tired. I know it. I am too. I think I know a way we could get on in, where we could do our own thing away from them others. Through the back. Everybody always go through the front, up the steps 'n shit. They don even know there another way. But we got to move real quiet."

Thirty meters farther Rosen held up his hand again. "We too high up. Better do the rest of the way on our belly."

Rosen set down the yogi, then laid himself down full-length on the cold sod. He turned his head to the yogi.

"Ya see what I'm doin, bro? Yawl do the same."

The yogi and the rest of the band spread themselves on their stomachs on the ground and single file slunk after Rosen in the direction of the church. They crawled silently as they could, but several of the brothers and sisters smelled real strong, and it wasn't long before the Dobermans picked up the scent and set to howling and lunging against the tier restraints. The church-goers were alerted, some of the men-folk separated from their women and, cupping their hands over their eyes, glared into the distance. But they didn't look down, and Rosen and his band were low as fungi. They kept on crawling, but the way wasn't easy. The hard soil was blistered with stone and spiky growth and fragments of broken glass. Crusted-over sores bled, old bruises pained, the beggars made a deep, long impression in the ground, bloody...

Rosen, who had been in more near-death situations than he could count on his fingers and toes too, couldn't make it out. The church kept receding. Or maybe the broken ground was on casters pushing them back as they crawled forward. Or the whole thing was in his black biblical head and he had wildly miscalculated the distance they had to go. Some shit was happening—they must have been crawling for a couple of hours at least and still had made no ground. Hell, they had to have made ground! Rosen could make out their belly-spoor twisting back way behind them for as far as he could see. His people were struggling. He held up his hand.

"Les hold it up for a minute. Rest."

They stopped.

"What you think, yogi?"

The Hindu gazed at him.

"Except for the hurtin pain, it feel like it ain us a-tall. That jive church, them pink asses out front, the bunch of us crawlin on our belly. It's like I'm seein it in a pitcher or on a wall. Like it's frozen cause it not *suppose* to change—"

"Avalokiteswara," the yogi said.

"Wuzzat? What you say?"

"Avalokiteswara is bodhisattva of mercy. Guiding spirit of pagoda. I will sing."

The yogi sang. Of course he had been singing almost without cease since Rosen had taken him under his wing. Only this time Rosen actually listened to the strange words. Sure enough he heard that long name the yogi had mentioned. He heard it repeated even as he motioned for the band to continue, and while they crawled he heard the weird name repeated again and again into his ear. They were making headway, the church no longer receded, they were crawling toward it, into the grassy hallowed ground enclosing it. The dogs continued to bark, but without heat. The men-folk, their hands visoring their eyes, continued to glare. Without sight. They were ornaments, roof-spouts, figures frozen in the attitude befitting them. Whereas Rosen's band wheezed and was alive and dragged its crooked, crooked length...

A circular steel door set in the grass behind the church, to the left of a yew: a sewer cover or oubliette, narrow as a spelunker's fissure, lead-heavy. Two of the brothers help Rosen lift it. The beggars slide silently under one at a time, the Ethiopian last...

Muted light, scented air, song. Nekkid girls.

Rosen grabs hold of the yogi's frail shoulders, chuckles. "This is what you wanted, ain it, brother? UNDERBELLY!"

UNDERBELLY
(2)

UNDERBELLY (2)

(41)

Jesús wakes hard.

(40)

Thirteen windowholes surround a center. Muted light, clayey smell. In the center's center a plush red velvet platform revolves against the clock. Weird petals spread: Ms. Harriet...

(3)

CLICK: "All-News" radio knocks up Wm. Tao-Jones, yesterday's closing (he already knows it), the traffic, the weather—he's up. He yawns. He yawns again. He mumbles, "Oh damn." Jesús still tired, but he is hard, man! He don't really want to jack off. No woman! His groinmind says UNDERBELLY. Wm's wife asleep, open-mouthed beneath the twisted sheets. She makes a sound—a sharp intake of breath, followed by a within-the-throat burble. Wm makes for the bathroom: first the sharp shaving light, then the radio again. All-news...

(8)

Rahman works in a fixit shop on Charles Street. TV's, typewriters, air-conditioners. Rahman repairs typewriters mostly, he is not particularly good at it. Tomorrow one of the fixit shop malingerers will call him "a Hindu fuck," meaning to be funny. Rahman is from Bangladesh, is Muslim. Doesn't matter. Gals change, the dance continues...

(15)

Jesús in his skivvies on his cot, sipping from a can of Schaefer, smoking a cigarette. Still hard. Can't do nothing about it, man. Not here. Lula, the Tijuana Buttercup, Loretta Kazoom, Raquel Walsh, Honeysuckle Benign, Suki U., Ms. Harriet...When the others do it—and some of them can do it!—the space still a-buzz with

(24)

Ms. Harriet. Child-noise.

(25)

Jesús lives in a single room on the fourth floor of a pre-war tenement on 49th Street off Ninth Avenue. At Ninth Avenue and 47th he stops to phone his mother. She lives on 111th and Madison. A neighbor answers the phone which is in the hall, knocks on her door... "Mamá, Jesito. Que tal, Mamá? Te quiero. I love you. No, I dint found nothin. Fantástico. Everything's okay. Me vengo más tarde. I see you later for dinner. Why don't you tell Soledad from upstairs to come too. Tell her Jesús be there. Tell her I found work real soon. Love to see her. Tiene bastante? You got enough beans, Mamá?"

(7)

Ms. Harriet is crucial. "All-News" dispensing Tao Wm applies the styptic. Four commercials, the weather, three commercials, the traffic report: twenty minute delays on the Long Island Railroad out of Westbury. "Oh damn!" Thick-skinned, saturnine, sleepy, wide-apart glossy black eyes. Rahman. Large family: pushed out of Bengal kin '71. Five brothers, two sisters. Tenant farmers, coax wheat out of the made-bad earth.

(6)

Child-noise. Wm pulls at his wife. "Fran, Billy is crying. I can't tend to him now. I've got to get going. Fran, you're going to have to stop swallowing those valium. Can you hear me?" Other space upstairs. I'm talking about UNDERBELLY. That space different. Pretty good action. Ms. Harriet did her thing there a few times. Wasn't the same as below. Below a tighter space. Friendly. Funky. Wishbone. Meadow... Choose your own word.

(4)

Isaac didn't wake cause Isaac didn't sleep. No way! Had better shit to do. "Ain't that right, baby?" Languidly: "Uh huh." "Whatchoo doin? Don't tell me you want more! Whatchoo made of, baby? Yeah, you jus slide on over here nice and close tell ole Isaac whatchoo made of. Thas right. You whisper it right...there."

(21)

A few words about Wm you'll say you know him. Late thirties, taut around the eyes, two Fords, paying out a "ranch house," lives in Westbury, works on Wall, a child, a bored tense wife, recently bought a pair of jogging shoes. Ms. Harriet there now. She is and she ain't. Point is UNDERBELLY don't stop. Rosen won't let it...

(2)

Finally Isaac slept. His woman left for work at 7:45, a nurse's aide at Mt. Sinai Hospital. Isaac conked right out. Was due at his own job— subway custodian on the Seventh Avenue IRT at 14th Street—at seven a.m. No sweat. What has she got? A slender long back, firm nice breasts, high fine rump, a pair of nuts, and a nice sized cock. Uncircumsized. Somewhat darker than the rest of her body. Young "girl," nineteen, twenty.

(13)

Rosen: "Gentmen, whisper what you want to Ms. Harriet, what you need. She can suc-cor you, don't matter how you say it, gentmen, Spanish, English, Urdu, Hebrew, she's a linguist, long tongue, pink bellysucker. Tell her what you want..."

(23)

Jesús ain't got shit. Whole lot of curly oily hair, whelped in P.R., lifts weights, drinks beer for breakfast, more beer and cuchifritos for lunch, a sweet ice, no job, thirty-one years old, digs the chicks. Ms. Harriet got that extra.

(33)

Lula ain't bad except she's so tall. Looking through the hole all you can see is up to her navel. Maybe a little tit when she bends. Isaac's forty-eight. Has a pot like a bowling ball, round, real hard. The rest of him's muscle I mean from his shaven head to his horny toenails. He slept for four hours and woke up hungry. Went out, had hisself three hot dogs, some soda, then two of them Greek things look kinda like hot dogs, a coupla beers. This was on Eighth Avenue seeing all the hookers was getting him horny. Rosen dangles UNDERBELLY at him. Not really. Isaac knows it, been there before six, eight times. Rahman's been there a lot, after work, on his days off. Wm squeezes in about an hour, no more, after Wall, then scoots down to Penn Station, catches the LIRR back. Often wishes he didn't have to, that he could stay in his booth, bent to his window, feeling soft and hard and soft and...Ms. Harriet. Rosen told him not to, told him: do it here, go home then and do it there with what you've spent on Ms. Harriet.

(28)

Rosen told him nothing. To speak of. Cavalier

(14)

Rosen did something quaint. Hired a yogi, bony little dude with a wide mobile mouth, had him stand in a corner, arms stretched in an upside down V above his head, one leg folded across the other thigh, wearing nothing but a loin cloth. In a corner of Ms. Harriet's space, while she did her thing. The yogi sang, or droned, soft, in some weird kind of language. And while he sang he grinned. Ms. Harriet dug it, maybe she even asked for it. Jesús there first. Hell, he ain't never left. In the toilet trying to piss. It's hard cause he still kinda hard. Isaac comes in. Rosen sends Wm in too. Wm carrying his attaché case with his *Wall Street Journal* and shit inside. Brown man pissing, black man waiting to piss in the cramped space scare Wm he backs out quick. Bumps into Rahman who doesn't notice got to take a piss. Rosen laughs. The music's loud and like you want it. Rosen spiels: "She's young, she's gorgeous, she's got a third laig. One quarter, gentmen, you can see what she's got. And since there ain't no glass on your hole you can do more than see. Hey, she's Harriet! She's on fire! She suc-cors you! She'll give you a long surprise, gentmen. Loosen your britches go on in. Twenty-five cent..."

(5)

Jesús likes number 3. It's a little off-center, but the mechanism on the window's broke. You put your quarter in, the window rises. Two minutes later, time gone, the window shuts, but not completely if you stick something underneath. Hard to see through the narrow slat, but ain't bad. And it don't cost. Only problem is Ms. Harriet can't look back watch your face as you pound it. When Jesús bout ready he stick another quarter in…Isaac's there, number 5. Wm's number 4. Jesús who already got off two loads, number 3. Rahman's number 2. All the other booths taken too. Always are with Ms. Harriet.

(34)

Lots of redneck kibitzers where Rahman works, fixit shop, neighborhood bungs. In the clutter Rahman at a typewriter. "How's it going? Gettin any? I mean white pussy. I know you like it cause I seen how you look at it. You gettin any, you Hindu fuck ya?" Laughter. No, it's the toilet flushing. Jesús finally pissed. Now Isaac. Jesús squeezes past Wm in the cramped space, past Rahman. But the door won't open… Ms. Harriet's pink where she should be. Her hair is real thick, "titian," long almost down to her rump. Her bush hair more orange than brown. Loves to boogie. Some of the others—Loretta Kazoom, the Tijuana Buttercup—they do it for the bread. Looking at them spread's like looking at gorse in winter. They never eyeball the dudes, don't smile at them. Look at the ceiling or someplace. Suki U is good. Raquel Walsh is good when her head is together. Same with Honeysuckle.

(9)

Okay, dudes in their booths bent a little to their windowholes. Ms. Harriet's space the color of sunset. The yogi standing in the corner with his foot in his crotch pokey little smirk on his face kinda singing. Ms. Harriet's lips moist and red her tongue a pink long fish she's circling grinning straight-legged she bends for the yogi. Buttocks glimmer pinkhole for the yogi tweaks his nose real friendly. She dangles toward Wm knows how he likes it front and titty lots of mom in the teeth is Wm's meadow also

(31)

Cock: "Ya wan some of this here, Bil-ly?" Jesús, next hole, observes laughs. His larger than "hers." In his fist, laughs. Harriet to Jesús: "Whatcha got for me, ba-by?" "Tungsten motherfuckin steel what I got." Ms. Harriet looking down his window-hole: "You ain't a-kidding! Gimme some then Jesito baby right here" (girlpink bung beneath cojones); Jesús smells her Isaac

(12)

Laughs. Booth 2 Rahman tickles himself Muslim through his pants saturnine real serious. Circles Ms. Harriet his way. Silently. Tongue-cobra, eyes, life-of-their-own hips, drone to Rahman. No chit-chat. Secret conch. Rahman's browner than Wm, whiter than Jesús than Isaac. Years working up there's Rahman Jesús Wm Isaac. Height working down: Wm Isaac Rahman Jesús. What else you want to know? Together quite a pudding, thank Ro Zen: discovered Harriet, unearthed the yogi, contrived the sunset.

(30)

Tungsten in the toilet trying to piss. Isaac comes in, only one commode. "How you?" "Whus happening, man?" Wm opens door brown man pissing black man waiting. Rahman got to—pushes open the door. All four there. Rosen dangles the yogi. No, not yet. Slams the door. Wm real scared his rites of pissage. Makes top dollar. MBA from Wharton. Wasp fam, wasp wife, lineage bones (Phila., Connecticut), Holyoke wife, good scotch, doesn't mount her much but dreams. Cheever-fodder don't feel sorry for that

(10)

Wasp.

(22)

Ms. Harriet powdering her parts. Pink big puff. Honeysuckle says: "Can I touch it, Harriet? Can I touch it just once?" Loretta Kazoom laughs. Suki U laughs. "Hey, it's heavy. It's a fucking handful..." Isaac woke to just outside Natchez. First bad fight when a cracker talked out nasty at his sister, Isaac fifteen jumped down his bicycle nearly killed the motherfucker bout as old as his daddy too. Came north: Detroit, later D.C. Two brothers, three sisters, just him and a sister still...grinding. Isaac: "What's happening?" Jesús: "Fuckin door jammed." "Use your foot, man, kick the motherfucker." Jesús kicks, don't open. Isaac: "Hang on"—tucks his pork. "Ain't no fuckin room in here." He kicks the door, no good. "Ain't that a bitch! Who you?" "Me? Wm." "What aboutchoo?" "Rahman." Isaac: "Listen up! Now we all gonna have to hit the motherfuckin door together..."

(26)

Rosen ex Machina finds a booth changes into Ms. Harriet. Better, finds a knife whittles his self into Ms. Harriet. Sticks his beak in the long sore his dream sucks out Ms. Harriet. Noseflute. Ro's a bitty little dude humped tribal scars or shit either side of his head Ms. Harriet ripens on velvet displays to us…conduits.

(11)

spic/jig/wasp/muslim. cramped john their foxhole. mortar fire Rosen's funky-butt music Harriet do the boogie. their faces mudfilthy can't tell black from brown from white. cocksize don't matter nor money. they wants to live and eat and love all over Ms. Harriet. death is the muvva of beauty. smallself peels fum their person like plaster. death is the muvva

(37)

Jesús on one knee drawing in the sand. A circle. "This here," he says, "is UNDERBELLY. Ms. Harriet this smaller circle in the middle. She never stops boogie she always there. Dig on her with your eyes you won't see nothin else. She feel so good you don't want to." Someone asks: "Where this at, bro? Puerto Rico?" Jesús: "Thas right." Fact is the toilet door won't open no way. Except there's another way through the commode. The shithole. Wm sees it first, says, "Fellas, look at this!" They send Rahman down there first hear him whoop it from the other side. Jesús then. Isaac. Wm. It's music and their secret spacehole wide open in her meadow sunset: Ms. Harriet. Rosen laughing: "Welcome home, gentmen. You seem a wee bit younger. She has a middle laig you watch please her sphinxter sigh tell me how you like the music."

(35)

Ms. Harriet on one knee on her velvet platform. Other leg spread right angle ass up open smile behind her shoulder for Rahman. The soft light laves the smooth floor, grass, "astro-turf." Sunset, game over, boosters gone, cars gone, stadium stripped of bodies. Sun going down, game over, play not over. Bloat Rosen swallows the cir-cum-scribed space. Wm swallows. Isaac. Rahman, Jesús. Rosen's chosen swallowing they pump their wellhead, weapon, firehose…discharge a kind of light in the littered stadium, a desperate grass. Soul-fenced. Ms. Harriet. UNDERBELLY. Ro

(32)

Zen dream-palace. Once a time ago Wm copped it from behind. In ocean tumbling from the train, kept him up, afloat. Rosen puts it to you: "Were Jesús himself less big, would he still love her?" Twenty past six. Four rubes locked in the toilet. Isaac on one knee maps his strategy on a sheet of toilet paper. "Dig it, me and Jesús hit it wif our shoulder from this side here. Whitestuff, you hit it from the other side. You Rahman kick the mother from the center. Wif your heel, hear! Ready? NOW!" Nothing. Wm's tremulous tenor: "Fellas, look at *this!*" The very shithole. They flush Wm down there first...

(36)

You want some dope on Ms. Harriet. She was suckling a noctule baby bat in Wales one starving June when Rosen found her. It's a true story it isn't where he found her. What can Rosen tell you? Stamen and petzel. Sturm and dong. All the gusto you can gets. If he says it fat and clear they'll say it's no good literature. The clit that got away. Naw, really. She's good people. Leave it at that.

(38)

The yogi putzed her.

(16)

Isaac has hisself a sweet ice he feeling kinda horny. Rahman eating curry or pilau in a South Asian restaurant on Carmine Street. Crappy food he doesn't notice. This Muslim's a slow beast. Rich fine Dravidian skin, sleepy wide-apart black eyes. Well-proportioned thick-skinned body. Has a room on Washington Street, sleeps there, eats there, doesn't hear the traffic. Doesn't precisely dream. Where does Ms. Harriet touch him?

(19)

Lula said she saw it. Ms. harriet circled past the yogi, with a quick flick undid his breechcloth, settled down bunger on him, he just stood there with his goddamn foot in his hip, smirking in that way of his, Ms. Harriet took him full, her pork did a stutter step, a little jig...The others saw, they was watching from the booths.

(18)

Rahman shot a bucketful. Ms. Harriet bends her ear to Rahman's hole to Wm whispers, "You were way the fuck out there, weren't you, baby? And everyone thought you was celebrating Christmas." Isaac booth number 5 hears this hearing something other. His woman finishes at Mt. Sinai, returns to her flat, Isaac not there. Hands on her hips: "Where he at?"

(27)

I'll be honest with you she's not all that gorgeous. I mean Ms. Harriet. The Tijuana Buttercup has her on looks. Some folks say Suki U has her too. Ms. Harriet's got that extra I'm not talking here about her nice fine muscle. It's not easy to put into words. Rosen's been trying to get it across to you in his own way. And he's closer to her than anybody—or was until she took off on him. Rosen himself? He's a brooding little dewlap with a big head and a whole lot of boils or shit on his stomach. Tribal scars. I'm joking. If I was to describe him to you from like his toenails to his head there wouldn't be no Ms. Harriet. Without her you could forget about the fist-humpers, soulchaff, the losers' brigade in five fucking colors. Them gone there ain't no

(17)

UNDERBELLY. Jesús there first. Except for the yogi. Big head, pock-marked belly, he stands in the corner like a freakin statue, one skinny leg folded across the other thigh, arms stuck above his head in an inverted V... Rahman on one knee on the dirty wood floor of the fixit shop: "This mechanism, it looks like a bird. You fit this bird into this other piece looks like a...nest." Looks up over his shoulder with slow menhir eyes.

(20)

Rosen on his side takes up about as much room as a coon curled dead in the road. Except for his kingfisher head and bloat pocked stomach. He's a vegetarian can't find no food in the vinyl city. Spread a white cloth over his face and knees. Protect his ears from striving brothers. Let him dream of gourds his Whitsuntide. Prick his thigh bray his body get somebody new in there. Raise the prime interest rate do it again to muzak. Twist him like a fetus bardo tongue to belly have him suck out Ms. Harriet. Use your trocar keep the lid on spending. Looks even dumber dead than before his bloat belly keeps on

(29)

Dreaming...Fran (of Wm and Fran of Westbury) prepares dinner her hands tremble. Rosen erecting a place for her:

(1)

Jesús dies big.

NOTE:
The numerals (41) within parenthesis apply to an alternate way of arranging the "panels." Several other arrangements are possible too, since the panels are portable, variable. Try it with dice...

CORA NAKED

(for M.J.)

CORA NAKED

*Lionel Bent in London, Boston, New York...sets down the phone,
turns on the phone-recorder:*

> VOICE (dulcet): Hello.
> BENT: Yes. Hello, can you tell me about your services?
> VOICE: Well, what would you like to know?
> BENT: What you...do. Also what you charge.
> VOICE: Okay. We lick, hick and stick. We'll also bake your stick.
> It depends on how much you want to spend. Rates—

Bent turns off the recorder, places a record on the phonograph
(Blind Lemon Jefferson), slips out of his clothes, goes into the bathroom.

*L.B. in Honduras, Zimbabwe, Timor...slips into his surplice or
gown, admits his first patient, the torturer, Sergeant Hean.*

> HEAN: It hasn't gotten any better, doc.
> L.B.: The headaches...
> HEAN: Worse than before. When I got to the compound last night
> this one gook still hadn't let on. Bloody sod! I knew it at once. What I
> mean is I could tell by the screams that we had gotten past the baths
> and into the electricity. My head was bursting with it. Still is.

Bent in the shower is thinking about Cora while he is listening to
Memphis Slim, six-feet-six in his stocking feet. Why is it that so many
of the male blues singers—the real ones—are big dudes? Leadbelly,
Howling Wolf, Slim, Big Joe Turner, Big Bill Broonzy...Bent is soap-

ing himself scrupulously. Cora likes him fragrant. Once she called him her "fragrant sandalwood recluse." Bent has become hard thinking of it. He gets out of the shower, dries himself, turns over the record. From outside: the skirl of an ambulance.

HEAN: Can't you do anything for me, doc?

L.B.:   Not unless you can come here on a regular basis. And you'd have to leave your job to do that, wouldn't you?

HEAN: I can't leave my job, doc. It's about the only thing I'm good at.

L.B.:   But you hate what you're doing.

HEAN (scratching his head):   It's not that. The pay's good. (Becoming angry) I just wish those buggers weren't so bleeding stubborn.

L.B.:   What is it you want, then?

HEAN: I want some of the same lot as before, doc. Only stronger.

Lionel Bent is lying on his back on the rug listening to Howling Wolf and thinking of Cora naked. Tonight he will finish installing the mirror above her bed. He opens the yellow notebook filled with verses, early drafts written in pencil, and turns to his most recent poem called "Cora Naked." It is a sestina and the critical words are: mirror, Cora, vinyl, carrion, death, and scuttle. Bent ruminates, pencil in his teeth...

This morning the torturer is combative. He presents L.B. with an item from a Rhodesian weekly. He has heavily underscored these words: "The black African makes virtually no use of his frontal lobes. All the particularities of black African psychiatry can be put down to frontal laziness. The so-to-speak normal black African is, in effect, a lobotomized European."

HEAN: What do you think of that?

L.B.:   I don't think anything of it.

HEAN: I've always wanted to ask you this: how does it feel being a black psychiatrist in a white country?

L.B.:   The country is predominantly colored, Sergeant. It is white-occupied.

HEAN: What are you trying to say?

L.B. (pause):   Why are you so angry this morning?

Bent turns off the record player and turns on the tape recorder. After

a few moments he jots something in his notebook, crosses it out, adds
a word or two. He is working on his sestina entitled "Cora Naked." As
he writes he recites into his tape recorder. The phone rings. It is his
answering service dunning him for the previous month's unpaid bill.
Bent hangs up the phone and turns on the TV. A woman he knows is
an actress in one of the afternoon soaps. He turns from one soap to
another for about ten minutes until he spots her. Her spun gold hair is
plaited on top of her head and she is wearing a nurse's outfit. She has a
petulant lower lip. Her lips are glossed, her yellow shining hair is
plaited. Bent removes his trousers...

HEAN: I can't stand the bleeding rain.
L.B.:   What's wrong with the rain?
HEAN: For one thing the gooks are all forced into this single cell
which is damned close to our own quarters. The other cells leak, you
see. They leak, and we don't want the gooks to catch pneumonia and
die on us. Not die like that. So they're forced together in this small cell
quite close to our own quarters, and they stink and they moan —
L.B.:   How many are there?
HEAN: Where do you mean?
L.B.:   In the small cell. When it rains.
HEAN: Twenty-five or thirty. The cunting cell is smaller than
your office. It's not even half the size of this small office of yours.
L.B.:   I see.
HEAN (taking hold of the psychiatrist's wrist):   I can't bleeding
take it, doc.
L.B.:   The stink or the moans?
HEAN (still clasping L.B.'s wrist and staring at him now apprais-
ingly):   You're not mocking me, are you, doc?

The actress with the plaited shining hair wearing the nurse's outfit is
in fact Cora. Her name in the soap opera is Jenny Boyd. She is not a
good actress. That is, she is a good deal better than the imbecile
material. In any case the half-hour segment is mercifully over. Bent
turns off the TV, sits down at his electric typewriter and commences to
type his sestina called "Cora Naked." Carrion, vinyl, Cora, mirror,
scuttle, death... When this is done he picks up the phone and dials the
Copying Center. A recording answers. Bent hangs up and dials again;
this time a functionary answers, says, yes, they will certainly be able to

Xerox six copies of his single page at around 6:45. Bent hangs up. He intends to present his sestina to Cora. The Cora in his sestina is dark-complected with pitch black hair. Bent, you see, does not wish to distort the legend, and Pluto, in Bent's reconstruction, is a kind of big black delta bluesman who might just shoofly pie with a fancy blonde—but would hardly choose to live with one on a semi-regular basis. Not down there. For no good reason Bent's fingers smell. The two longest fingers of his right hand, it seems. He has some time. He drops a disc into the Betamax and observes himself naked emerge from his shower, semi-erect, carrying his tool chest. The mirror above Cora's bed needs mending. He gathers his dirty laundry, stuffs it into the laundry bag, goes out the door.

HEAN: I never told you what it sounds like, did I?

L.B.:   What's that?

HEAN: The screams. How it's different depending on where he's feeling it—

L.B.:   You told me—

HEAN: There are three main zones of access: the head and neck; the pelvis, front and back; and the soles and ankles. The vehicles we use—gloved fist, baton, heat, bath, electricity—can be efficiently applied to each of these zones. Except for the eyes, the progression is from either end of the body towards the pelvis. The eyes along with the genitals and rectum are reserved for the hard cases. In a like manner the screams become more intense and are in a higher register the closer the pain is to these critical areas: the eyes, the genitals and the rectum. This is to be expected, but there is something else, another... component to these screams that we didn't expect. Or I didn't. I don't know what the others feel, whether they hear these screams as I do. I never discussed it with them.

L.B.:   Why not?

HEAN: Why not! It just isn't done, that's why not. Let's say you were an anarchist and we had you at the compound and inserted an ionized cylinder up your prick, and afterwards, when we released you, you weren't able to get it up. Weren't able to get a proper hard-on. Would you be going all around mentioning this weakness of yours to the blokes? To your mates and so on?

Smelling richly of sandalwood soap (except for the fingers of his right hand), Bent is walking in the direction of Cora. On the northern wall of the Copying Center he sees this graffito: a figure comprised of squares and rectangles and brandishing a club, being fellated by a figure comprised of rectangles and squares. He enters the Copying Center and hands the small woman with the thinning hair his sestina. She glances at the title then looks up at him. I found it, Bent explains, beneath a 1951 Edsel. I'm delivering it to the local Moral Majority office for processing. She is wearing designer jeans. Bent thinks about what he will do tonight. To Cora. While he waits he studies a two-page spread on ithyphallic stereo components in *Playboy*. He sets down *Playboy* and picks up a back copy of *Audubon*. A young beggar thrusts his head in the doorway, wanting alms. Us beards got to stick together, he tells Bent. Under his matted hair the beggar is wearing miniature ear-phones. What kind of music are you listening to? Bent asks. All-news, the beggar says. I'm listening to all-news radio. Lionel Bent, "Cora Naked" in his rucksack, is walking. He has washed his hands in the washroom of the Copying Center, and now he is walking. Hang in there, Cora. Stay moist for your fragrant sandalwood recluse.

HEAN: Where are you from, doc?

L.B.:   Martinique.

HEAN: What made you come to this godforsaken place? Don't tell me. There are damned few places where a black psychiatrist can hang out his shingle, right?

L.B.:   How is your headache this morning?

HEAN: What is it with you anarchists? I don't mean you personally, doc. Those wogs at the compound. One ducked out on us last night.

L.B.:   Escaped?

HEAN (laughs):   Died. The sod died on us. Not unusual, mind you. Cock of it was we were closing in on him. We were damned close to bursting this *Maquis* bit of theirs wide open.

L.B.:   How did it happen?

HEAN: What's that?

L.B.:   How did he die?

HEAN: The arse—pardon my Afrikaans. Ionized cylinder in the front, chemist's bath in the rear. One of the lads turned the hose too high. Ruptured the inner tube like—the wog's I'm talking about. And you bleeding ask me if my head aches!

L.B.:   What was his name?

HEAN: Whose name?

L.B.:   The murdered prisoner.

Bent ejects the video disc and puts Big Mama Thornton on the record player. Naked he moves from room to room gathering his dirty laundry. What's this: a pair of magenta lace panties under the Betamax? Cora would be leaving the studio about now, escorted to her taxi by Brad, the young doctor lead in the soap. He has khaki hair and a cleft chin. In his intern's smock he resembles an early Christian in a Hollywood movie. He opens the cab door, waits for leggy Cora to settle in, closes the door, then slips into the front and vrooms cross-town, maneuvering the wheel with one long hand—Bent ejects this disc and moves into the bathroom to wash his hands. Somehow— emptying the kitty litter?—his fingers have picked up something foul. Ball and chain. The old *Audubons* are a great deal better than the recent ones with their ads for Exxon and Mobil and Xerox and Mercedes Benz. The issue that Bent holds in his hand has a gannet in flight on the cover and dates from 1968. Sirens from the street. Lionel Bent appraises himself in the full-length mirror. He must not forget his tool chest. He straps the explosives to his chest and goes out the door locking two of the four locks behind him.

L.B.: What's with the urinary tract now?

HEAN: Retaining piss, doc. Can't seem to get it all out.

L.B.: Since when is this?

HEAN: Nearly a fortnight, I'd say.

L.B.: That would be around the time the prisoner was murdered, wouldn't it?

HEAN: You keep saying murdered. I have a feeling you don't approve of our tactics, doc. Not approving is your bundle, but when you din it about...I don't want you to get in trouble, doc.

L.B.: You can't urinate without discomfort?

HEAN: There's some pain. Not that much. I just can't seem to get it all out.

L.B.: Does the urine give off a strong odor?

HEAN: Yes. That worries me. You see I did a bit of fucking.

L.B.: Oh?

HEAN: Not with the Mrs., is what I'm saying. That same night— after the gook ducked out. Three or four of the lads and me—we went to the Delta—

L.B.: Ibo Delta?

HEAN: What of it! We needed a bit straightaway.

L.B.: Urinate in one of the paper cups in the loo and leave it with the nurse on your way out. We'll know in about a fortnight.

Bent straps the radio-recorder about his waist, fits the ear-phones over his ears and goes out, locking one of the four locks behind him. He is listening to all-news radio, and even as the ripe-toned meteorologist is forecasting fair weather—it has begun to rain. Acid rain, it looks like. Cora's warm bed will be a godsend. But what about the mirror? The mirror above her circular bed needs mending and the only tool Bent carries is the nine inch zinger in his side pocket. After examining a graffito stencilled on the side of the building, Bent drops his laundry in the laundromat, exchanging smiles with the youngish proprietress. Magenta, magenta, he whispers into her small ear. I can't hear you, she shouts. With her slim hand on the small of his back she is coaxing him into the vestry—Bent ejects this disc and stretches out on the carpet. His fingers smell. He reaches into the drawer and withdraws a sprig of rosemary. That's a thought: he adds a phrase containing the word "rosemary" to his sestina, substituting "rosemary" for "vinyl." This of course means recasting the entire sestina. After reflecting a moment, he puts back "vinyl." It is ten minutes past four. He inserts the same disc he has just ejected: Come into the vestry, she whispers, her breath smelling interestingly of Chlorox. Did you bring the bracelets? Bent lays them on the dryer and crosses his wrists behind his back. As he walks he observes the clouds, cumulonimbus alternating with cirrostratus. It is a holiday of some kind: teenagers wearing crash helmets are coursing through the street. Bent hasn't yet eaten. He can't eat now, in the acid rain, with his hands cuffed behind his back. No matter, he'd just as soon not bring those villainous-smelling fingers to his face.

HEAN: Good news, doc. The headaches have stopped, and I'm back to pissing good. We got one of the older wogs to pigeon, you see. We know now just about all we have to know about the terrorist *Maquis*. I can promise you that there won't be a single rutting black terrorist *Maquis* by this time tomorrow morning.
L.B.: I see.
HEAN: You don't look very happy about it, doc.
L.B.: I got your report back from the laboratory.
HEAN: What's that?
L.B.: General paresis, Sergeant.
HEAN: I'm not reading you.
L.B.: Tertiary stage syphillis. Your cortex has about had it.
HEAN: That nigger wog bitch—
L.B.: Your pathology is of long standing, Sergeant. Fifteen, even twenty years.

HEAN: I don't believe it. That pissing business was the only symptom.

L.B.: This specific pathology is occasionally symptom-free. In the first two stages. Have a look at the laboratory report on my desk.

HEAN (picks up the report): I can't cypher this rot.

L.B.: Repeat after me, Sergeant: Methodist Episcopal. Meth-od-ist E-pis-co-pal.

HEAN: Mephistoph...

Even with his hands behind his back Bent can smell them. He is stopped by a National Guardsman in a surgical mask holding a bayoneted rifle across his chest. You can't come through here. Why not? Bent asks. Wipe-out, the Guardsman says through his surgical mask. Store-front church bombed. Five-alarm job. Didn't you hear the engines? Anyone hurt? Bent asks. You better believe it. Hundred or more. We're pickin' up the pieces right now. Been doin' it since 7:30 this morning. Bent is thinking of Cora. Better put something over your face, buddy. Wriggling out of her nurse's outfit, then her magenta lace panties, she drops the fragrant pile on the carpet, circles toward him. How did it happen? Guardsman shrugs: Seems some of these blacks were working on an incendiary device and messed up. Incendiary device? In the church? The Guardsman laughs: They had a whole fucking arsenal in the cellar from what I hear. Mirror, Cora, vinyl, carrion, scuttle, death. Bent closes the blinds, bolts the door, and turns on the tap in the bath. The phone rings: it is the answering service— Bent ejects this disc. He is watching the festivity through his window: teenagers with ball bearings in their fists which they are clicking loudly, rhythmically, are coursing through the street in tandem, blankfaced, six abreast...

HEAN: They haven't gotten any better, doc.

L.B.: The headaches?

HEAN: Worse than before. At the compound last night this one wog still hadn't let on. You know how unstable the electric current is in this godforsaken desert. I couldn't apply the ionized cylinder efficiently—the bugger screamed. He made the devil's own din.

L.B.: It gave you a headache.

HEAN (narrowly): You're not mocking me, are you, doc?

Bent ejects this disc and picks up the back copy of *Audubon*. It dates from 1968 and has a photograph of a gannet in flight on the cover.

Cora, scuttle, vinyl, mirror, death, carrion. She is waiting in the warm circular bed, she won't understand. Bent has begun to run

HEAN: You know what it is, doc?

L.B.:   What's that?

HEAN: People like yourself. Why can't these black terrorist *Maquis* wogs look to people like yourself? We should all be better off, eh? Wouldn't you agree with me that it is a mistake to voodoo the people? You, despite everything, are *très comme il faut.*

"As if in protest to our intrusion," the naturalist writes, "the gannets gathered over us in absolute silence. It was like being watched by a multitude of intent, astonished children. They used the slight southeast wind to hover over us in a dense, frankly intimidating, mass." Bent is running

HEAN: You are, despite everything, respectable. Which is why I put it to you: Set an example, my dear doctor. In our small way we must all of us labor to offset the voodooing of the people. If only I could piss.

L.B.:   What's that?

HEAN: I'm retaining urine, doc. Can't seem to get it all out...

Bent is running

FEEL LOVE,
SOMETIMES

FEEL LOVE,
SOMETIMES

The game is called Hit-the-Sky-with-the-Tennis-Ball. The small humpbacked man with the large head and pronounced overbite is alone in the grassy field beneath a white wide sky. He wears black shorts, black and white high-topped sneakers, and a yellow tee shirt with 45 YEARS OF ANGST stencilled on the back. Holding a yellow tennis ball in one small fist, he shouts the name "Blaise Pascal!" and throws the ball high into the air. Pascal, head up, circling like a dog pursuing its tail, catches the ball in his tiny clasped hands.

Rosen makes the notation.

Next he shouts the name "H.P. Blavatsky!" and hurls his tennis ball so high that his sciatic nerve twinges. The rotund matron with the dignified mien, gazing straight ahead, does not budge until the final split second when she thrusts out a hand. However the ball hits her on her broad chest and falls to the ground.

Rosen appears unsettled—he makes his notation.

Above him the thick white cumulus clouds move almost imperceptibly from west to east. Rosen lowers his voice an octave, coarsens it, shouts the name "Cora Dance!" and hurls his tennis ball high into the air. The slight grey-haired lady circles conscientiously following the yellow ball's circuit, both hands outstretched... The ball falls several feet to her right. She is not even close.

Next to the name "Dance" Rosen pencils an "x."

This much of the dream is familiar: the game, the players (these naturaly rotate), and then the dream fades. But tonight there is this coda:

When the sweating Rosen gets back to his bicycle he sees that something—a brown paper bag—is stuck in the spokes of his rear wheel. Rosen extracts the bag, from which he removes a harmonica. At once this frame is replaced by another in which the harmonica has become an accordion. Rosen, harnessed uncomfortably within the cumbersome instrument, is trudging over unfamiliar terrain...

Rosen the following a.m. was sitting with his short legs on his desk, reflecting on his dream, when there was a knock at the door.

He said nothing.

The same sound—three medium loud taps, 3/4 tempo, a second time.

"Come in," Rosen said.

She had auburn hair, black quick eyes, and a wide mobile mouth. Age: 32-35.

Taking Rosen in, her eyes turned doubtful. She smiled ironically. "Don't tell me you're..." She didn't finish.

Rosen, removing his legs from his desk, gave her his lidded look.

"I suppose"—she was brazenly eyeing him up and down—"you *must* be."

"Why don't you..." Rosen's words were obscured by the shrieking of an ambulance siren.

Her bright black eyes were certainly analytic, but they were also myopic, Rosen decided, capable of misting over with feeling, passion.

"Why don't you sit down, Ms?"

She laughed suddenly, easily. "I will. Thank you."

She sat on the harder of the two chairs facing the desk, on the tip of the chair, torso straight, slender knees together. Rosen smelled her scent. She wore a purple cotton shift delicately embroidered with an orange fleur-de-lys pattern, medium-heeled sandals, no stockings. No nail polish on slim toes or slim fingers. Almost no makeup on her handsome expressive face.

Rosen made his appraisal rapidly, imperceptibly, he thought.

She said, "What do you think? Do I," she cocked her head, "measure up?"

In fact she was unusually breasty for a slim (imperially slim) woman. Rosen said, "I take things in. It's my job."

"I see."

She was looking around. Motioning with her head to the book-laden shelves on either side of the room, she said, "I didn't think that a private investigator's readings went beyond *Field and Stream*. But, now that I think of it, there was," she smiled, "Dupin. Also Borges' sleuth—what was he called?"

"Erik Lönnrot," Rosen said.

"Yes, Lönnrot. I suppose, like them, you play at your work?"

Rosen smiled accomodatingly. She couldn't know that he was tired, in the process of giving up his "work." He was, though, alert enough to recognize in the woman's zany irreverence an aspect of her breeding. Bennington, '69, was Rosen's guess.

"Will you tell me your name?"

"Lila Evans Bent."

Rosen thought for a moment.

"My husband is Lionel Bent."

"The poet?"

She nodded her head with a kind of vehemence. A burnished strand of auburn hair shook free from her bun. "Yes, the poet," she said. "He gave that up."

"Gave it up?"

Lila Bent smiled ruefully. "Lionel published two books of verse—"

"*Freaks' Dreams*," Rosen recalled, "and..."

"And *Runes*."

"Yes, *Runes*."

"You read them?" Lila Bent asked.

"I did, yes. I thought several of the poems were exceptional."

Lila Bent with her brow knit was scrutinizing him to see whether he meant what he said. She nodded slowly.

The two slim volumes, Rosen recalled, had appeared a few years apart, the first six or eight years ago, and both had moved him very much. *Runes* was a continuation of *Freaks' Dreams*, and each poem was in effect a dream, dreamed by one kind of pariah or another: acromegalic giant, child molester, congenital syphilitic, circus dwarf, legless Vietnam veteran...Each "freak" uttered his askew dream to the reader in energetic, even spasmodic, cadences which were uncompromising and sometimes unnerving.

"And now?" Rosen asked.

"And now," Lila Bent crossed her svelte legs, "I am in this cloistral book-lined room conferring with Malcolm Rosen." She smiled. "You come, you know, highly recommended."

"I see. Can you tell me by whom?"

"By a female client of yours. She said you were hung like a horse."

Lila Bent laughed loudly. Her black eyes were shining. "Actually it was Lionel who mentioned your name a while back. He had read something about you in a journal. A Trotskyite journal."

"Troglodyte?"

"Trotskyite." She trained her fine ironic eyes on him.

"Ah, that would have been some time ago," Rosen said.

"Yes? And now?"

"Now and for some time past I have been," Rosen smiled, "disengaged."

Lila, also smiling, said, "You look like a charming orangutan when you grin. I think you will do very nicely."

"I see."

"Not yet, Malcolm Rosen. You'll see after I explain. But that will have to wait. I must leave now. Can we meet again? Day after tomorrow?"

"That's Thursday. Yes, I think so. Here?"

"No. I'd prefer to meet in the Museum of Modern Art. In front of Max Beckmann's *Departure*. At two o'clock. Is that all right?"

Rosen said it was. Lila Bent stood, gave him her strong slim hand, withdrew.

Though the weather appears mild, the diminutive humpback in the wide grassy field wears a yellow hooded sweatshirt with the hood fastened snugly over his head. ATMAN is stencilled on the front of his sweatshirt, BRAHMAN on the back. Hoarsely he utters the name "John Brown!", then flings his tennis ball high into the air...

When he returns to his bicycle it has become a kiln. He himself is gently but firmly accosted, his hood is removed exposing his shaven crown. Supple black hands withdraw a dagger (the word the priest uses is "misericord") which is sterilized in the kiln. One priest applies the misericord to Rosen's crown, then another, also black, rubs an herb into the fresh incision. The fragrance of the herb at once flooding through Rosen's body. The wonder of it awakens him —

Two prospective clients phone that afternoon; Rosen refuses both, explaining that he is winding down. In fact he is occupied with the Bents. His hunch is that his time will not be his own.

Rosen subways to the museum. A young black man shouldering a large radio-recorder sits across from him. He sets the burnished machine on his knees, removes a fried chicken breast from a fast-food package he is carrying, and opens his tabloid to *Help Wanted*. When, ten minutes later, Rosen stands to exit, the young man has turned to *Sports* and is eating a drumstick.

Rosen arrives at the museum at the appointed time, is informed that Beckmann's *Departure* is on the third floor, locates it. Three large oblong panels painted, according to the plaque, in Germany between 1933-35...

"Well?"

It was Lila's scent. She had come up behind him.

"Hello, Lila."

"Hello, yourself. What do you think?"

"About the painting?"

"Naturally."

"I admire it. It would take me some time to explain why."

"Lionel admired it too. He even wrote some words about it."

"Yes?"

"Yes. I'll show them to you. Let's have a drink."

Sitting in the museum garden over wine, Lila, her auburn hair braided behind her head, wearing a close-fitting maroon jumper (a silver-bordered yin-yang brooch pinned to one opulent breast), looked somewhat older, though no less lovely. She was watching Rosen in her appraising, ironic way.

"You're a droll sort of man, aren't you?"

"Am I?"

"I think you are. But can you laugh at yourself, Malcolm Rosen?" She smiled. "May I call you Malcolm?"

"Of course."

"Lionel laughed at himself quite a lot. It was a handsome quality in him, I always thought. It made it less hard for him to..." Lila didn't finish. Her eyes had suddenly welled with tears.

"What happened?" Rosen asked. "Where did your husband go?"

Lila was fumbling in her purse. She withdrew a small index card with writing on it.

"I found this in an art book which Lionel had been looking through."

She handed Rosen the card. The writing was in pencil in a small clear, perhaps painstakingly clear, hand.

Beckmann's *Departure*

An oblique but palpable horror. A somehow reasonable horror. Brutality, violence; a radically unreasonable violence and brutality. Yet rendered in a pastel-like oil which gives a permanent mineral cast to it, as though to say that horror, loveliness, cruelty, violence, contemplation finally are indivisible.

Rosen read these words again. He said, "Can I hold on to this for a while?"

Lila nodded.

"Won't you tell me about it, Lila?"

A strand of braid had come loose. She was nervously twining it around her finger.

"He left." She shrugged. "Almost seven weeks ago now. Took the bus to Miles City, Montana. I can't tell you why he chose Miles City, Montana, except that there are Sioux Indians there. Lakota Sioux, I believe. Lionel wanted to be there. He said he would write to me soon, and that he would return within a month."

"Did you believe him?"

"What do you mean?"

"Did he seem to be saying these things because he meant them, or to comfort you?"

Rosen's question appeared to surprise her. She considered it uneasily, pulling at her cuticles with her fingernails.

"I don't know," Lila finally said. Then, as if to justify that Lionel had meant what he said, she added: "He took almost no clothing. A few books and his mouth organ. That was about it."

"Mouth organ?"

"Yes. His harmonica. Lionel called it mouth organ. A simple little diatonic harmonica he picked up someplace. He played it quite a lot—I'm going to have another wine."

While Lila was motioning to the waitress Rosen made a few notations.

"What are you writing?" she said.

"Some of the things you're telling me. So that I can remember them. What kind of music did he play on his mouth organ?"

"Oh, this and that. Rhythmic stuff. Primitive-sounding, I suppose you'd call it."

Rosen sipped his wine. Behind Lila in the garden, Rodin's massive *Balzac* loomed...

"What are you thinking?"

"I was looking at the Balzac," Rosen said. "Art doesn't work now the way it did then."

Lila guffawed cynically.

"Your husband's books? Did they do at all well?"

"Do?" Lila said. "You mean 'sell.' No, of course not. Verse has not done well since Edna Millay. And it gets worse every half-hour. Lionel's books were remaindered less than a year after they were published."

"Ah."

"But then Lionel expected this."

"It didn't hurt him?"

"No, it *did* hurt him. But still he expected it. Lionel didn't write for that reason—critical acclaim, a wide audience. *Freaks' Dreams* and *Runes* exist because they were the only way for him to convey those things that haunted him."

Lila was focusing on Rosen with intense black eyes. His own eyes kept shifting to her yin-yang brooch.

"You approve of my tits, Malcolm?"

"Sorry. I was looking at your brooch."

"Lionel gave it to me."

"How long were you and he together, Lila?"

"Seven years. Nearly seven years. I had bought a copy of *Runes* in Barnes and Noble. Remaindered," she laughed. "After I read it I tried to get hold of the first book, but couldn't. His publisher said it was out of print. None of the libraries or book stores had it. Finally I wrote to Lionel in Maine. That was how we met."

"Ah."

"When we actually got together do you know the first thing I asked him?"

Rosen shook his head.

"I asked, 'Do you have hope?' "

Rosen waited.

"His reply was, 'I feel love.' He reflected for a moment, then added, 'Sometimes,' and laughed. We both laughed.

Lila was looking down at the table, blinking her eyes nervously. She said:

"Maybe the single pertinent criticism of Lionel's poems is that they lack laughter. Actually there are some very funny passages in both volumes. But they're rare. His feeling for his people is so urgent that other, attendant, emotions are subsumed."

Rosen nodded.

"And yet there were lots of readers," Lila said, "who felt nothing in the poems. To them Lionel's freaks were his private obsession and ought to have remained private."

"I see."

"Most of the notices were written by critics who felt this way, offended, assaulted by Lionel's passions. Even though Lionel wrote almost nothing about politics specifically, his intense concern for the—the disaffiliated must have seemed like insurrection to these people. Some of them loathed, violently loathed, his work."

"How did he react to those critics who violently loathed what he wrote about with such urgency?"

Lila finished her second wine. "Are you having another?"

Rosen shook his head.

"You're not in a hurry?"

"Not at all."

She ordered another white wine. The waitress came by with a carafe. When Lila raised the glass to her lips her hand was trembling.

"Malcolm Rosen: Tracer of Lost Persons." She laughed. "How long have you been committed to this odd profession of yours, Malcolm?"

"A long time."

"Successfully?"

Rosen considered. "Statistically, I've been modestly successful. Overall, though, I would not say I've done well."

"You sound tired."

Rosen smiled. "You're right." After a moment he added, "I've refused half-a-dozen clients in the last month. In fact your husband's...departure will be occupying all of my time."

"Your professional time, you mean."

Rosen shrugged. "I don't usually make that distinction—professional time, private time."

"Why this, Malcolm? What is it about Lionel that has gotten to you?"

Silence. Then:

"I'd say that it is a constellation of factors."

Lila cocked her head, assumed a grave demeanor, coarsened her voice, and mimicked: "a constellation of factors." She laughed. "What do you think of me?"

"Oh. I'd say you were variable."

"That's diplomatic of you, Malcolm." She laid her cool slim hand on his. "You asked about Lionel's reaction to unkind criticism. He said little about responses, good or bad, but the offensive responses pained him. Other writers—I'm thinking of Blake, Chekhov, Traven, Elsa Morante, writers whose concerns resembled Lionel's—they continued to write." She shrugged her shoulders. "Lionel stopped."

"Had he already stopped when you got to know him?"

"No, he was writing then. Though not for publication. There must be more than 100 pages of unpublished poems in his study."

"On the same general theme as his earlier books?"

"I can't tell you," Lila said. "He never showed them to me. No, that's not true. He did show me some of the first pieces he did. As for their resemblance to the published poems, I'll let you be the judge of that."

"All right. When did Lionel begin to play his mouth organ?"

Lila looked up from her glass. She seemed suddenly tipsy. "He had begun to play before we started living together. It picked up after a time. And then he began to play on the streets." Lila was absent-mindedly fingering the rim of her glass, producing a faint high tone. "Lionel would leave the house—we were in Maine then—walk to the railroad station, sit and talk with the oldtimers there, and play his mouth organ. When the house we rented was sold and we had to leave, I suggested we'd be better off in Boston or New York City. He would have preferred remaining in Maine. I guess I thought, or hoped, that the upbeat of the city would coax—if that's the word—him back to work. It didn't happen. He did write some, but not much really. And he pretty much gave up reading. Between us, oddly enough, things were somehow still good. We lived off the money in our savings, I worked as a librarian two or three times a week. We laughed. We made love..." She paused.

Rosen waited. Lila was gazing over his shoulder, probably at nothing in particular.

"There was," Rosen asked, "passion between you?"

She looked at him. "Yes. It was as good or better than ever. Lionel trusted me. Or—trusted me then."

"Yes. How long had you been living in the city when Lionel left?"

"Not long. A bit more than a year."

"And during that time he was playing his music where?"

"In the apartment mostly. Though he would sometimes play outside. Once someone mentioned seeing him north of Columbia—in Harlem actually—playing in the street. When I asked Lionel about this he laughed."

"Can you recount the conversation, Lila?"

"I asked him whether he had been playing his mouth organ in Harlem. And he laughed and said something like: 'Where isn't it Harlem?' "

"Hmm. Lila, I'm going to ask you a question that might sound insensitive. Can you point to a specific action—aside from your husband's poems and the harmonica playing—that would indicate his concern for the disadvantaged?"

"You must understand," Lila said softly, "that Lionel is not really a doer in the sense this word is generally used."

Rosen nodded.

"Of course he did many small things every day, but let me give you the specific action you asked for. Last winter—an unusually warm day in February—we were walking through the Bowery to Chinatown to have dinner when we saw this awful thing. Eight or ten gang members—teenage boys—were viciously taunting a derelict who was crumpled against some ruin of a building. They were holding lighted matches next to his hair, jabbing him with their shoes—when Lionel bolted across the street to intervene. At once these kids turned on him, kicking, beating him.

"I ran screaming into the street and stopped a truck. The driver got out, but in the meantime something terrible happened. One of the toughs doused the derelict with his own whisky and set him on fire. The truck driver radioed for an ambulance and when it came Lionel accompanied the burned man to St. Vincent's Hospital, remaining with him in the Emergency Room for most of the night. The burned man died. Lionel was severely depressed for days after this, though neither of us mentioned it again."

The familiar broad grassy field beneath a congenial sun. They are naked—the slender quick-eyed woman with the surprising breasts, and the small humped man with the large head. Rosen has mounted her from behind, is caressing her breasts with one outstretched hand, with the other is trying to locate the orifice. This he is unable to do... Finally he changes his position and insinuates his head between her thighs, finds at once the fragrant orifice, inserts (deliberately) himself, such a sweet tension—he is about to erupt. Instead he is tumbling head-over-heels down-mountain, unable to catch his breath, finally sliding to a stop in the scree. Slowly, resignedly, he rights himself, swipes perfunctorily at the ash and residue on his bruised body, settles his huge head on his shoulders, anchors his feet, commences the punishing trek up-mountain, Lila's elusive scent encompassing him...

The museum meeting with Lila was on Thursday. On Saturday Rosen receives in the mail the key to the Bent's apartment. That morning he subways to upper Broadway, locates the tarnished pre-World

War II building, rides the cramped elevator to the 16th floor, lets himself inside. A spacious flat: wide, high-ceiling living room, eat-in-kitchen, two good-sized bedrooms, one a study, separated by a bathroom. Except for the large number of books in tall wooden shelves, few furnishings. In the bedroom a queen-sized boxspring and mattress, two Navaho-type scatter rugs on the wood floor. A small desk and chair where, evidently, Lila works. On the walls framed reproductions: Klee, Dubuffet, Miro, Giacometti.

Lionel's study is more sparsely furnished still. A narrow wooden table and straight-backed kitchen chair in front of the window, an old Olivetti portable near the chair atop a wooden fruit crate. A standing lamp made of wrought iron. No rugs on the unpolished wood floor. On a wall four of Edward Curtis' portraits of North American Indians. No calendar, no clock.

Rosen sits on the chair and looks out the window to the sooty rooftops: smokestacks, TV antennas, rusted water tanks. In the distance, to the northeast, the arch of a bridge, perhaps the Triboro. Muffled sounds of traffic, the wail of an ambulance.

It is in the wooden crate that Lionel's papers are kept. Carefully Rosen withdraws several folders, none of which is labeled. The folders contain Lionel's poems interspersed with American Indian poems that have been previously published and are Xeroxed, with the name of the original journal in the upper left corner. Lionel's poems are themselves about American Indians. The title of each—Rosen is going through them one by one—is usually the name of an Indian—Black Shawl; Lame Deer; Hump; Crazy Horse—or the place name of a battle. Some are without titles. Most appear to deal with the tribes who lived in the northern plains or the northwest, and they are largely about privation. But the leaps and thrusts, the surges of feeling so evident in Lionel's two published books are absent here. Instead: notation, restraint, economy of utterance. Not acceptance, so far as Rosen can determine. Rather a colder, or at least a muted rage.

Beneath Lionel's poem, "Black Elk's Sacred Hoop," is a pencilled note: "Chekhov's 'Ward 6.'"

After leaving the flat Rosen makes his round of the bookstores and obtains a collection of Chekhov's stories in the fourth store he tries.

2

The following Monday, mid-morning, Rosen was sitting in the Trailways bus en route to Miles City, Montana. Near Albany a red-haired girl carrying an infant boarded the bus and sat next to Rosen.

She said her name was Ginny and that she was visiting her husband, Dennis, in an army base in Eau Claire, Wisconsin. Ginny and the child lived with her parents in Albany, and after Dennis received his training he would be returning to an army base near Albany. Ginny was a pleasant-faced young woman who emitted a sweet milky odor. She held and handled her infant, Dennis Jr., with a casual tenderness and seemed wholly at ease in the crowded bus.

Rosen recalled some lines from Whitman about the "mechanic's wife, babe at her nipple, interceding for all mankind." Something like that.

Humanity otherwise, as Rosen glimpsed it from his Trailways compartment, fared much less well. Despair, vapidity. Eighteen-wheel trucks discharging diesel. Suspicion, pride, vapidity. On the bus, though, Ginny's imperturbable red-haired trust and young white motherhood evoked light, sweetness in nearly everyone.

Rosen took out his copy of Chekhov and began reading "Ward 6." By the time the bus was pulling into Rochester he had finished the delicately modulated yet extraordinarily sympathetic story about a physician whose overwhelming compassion for his mental patients — and especially for one — becomes finally identification: he is himself netted.

Lila had given Rosen a small snapshot of her husband. Taken a few years before, it was, she said, the most recent photo she had. Neither of Bent's books had contained a jacket photo, and Rosen had no idea of how he looked until now. Clearly the photograph had captured an unwilling subject: his head is askew, one eye partially closed. A large man in a plaid shirt, dark tousled hair, thickly bearded. A rather broad, high-boned face. Though the contours of the head are roughly hewn, the countenance, the attitude, seem withdrawn, even frail. Rosen thought of photographs of the poet Robert Lowell. He recalled also a caricature he had seen many years ago of a burly fist cradling a lily; the caption read, HEMINGWAY.

Rosen looked again at Bent's comment on Beckmann's *Departure*:

> ...a radically unreasonable violence and brutality. Yet rendered in a pastel-like oil which gives a permanent mineral cast to it, as though to say that horror, loveliness, cruelty, violence, contemplation finally are indivisible.

That "permanent mineral cast" interested Rosen. He wasn't certain why.

Someone on the bus was strumming a guitar. Rosen, who had

closed his eyes, confused the tentative chords with the sound of a harmonica. Ginny touched him on the shoulder, then placed her infant in his arms. She was going to the lavatory. The child with the teething toy in his mouth regarded Rosen with a dreamy amphibian gaze.

Ginny returned. Rosen dozed; he dreamt, vaguely, of Indians; he awoke in Pennsylvania. Ginny was breast-feeding her child. Rosen could smell the milk. It resembled the fragrance in his dream of a few nights before, in which the "priest" had rubbed an herb into the top of his head.

The bus driver announced that they would be stopping for dinner. A restaurant off the thruway in Erie, Pennsylvania. Rosen sat at a table with Ginny, two elderly nuns, and a prematurely wizened, excessively talkative man in a yachting cap who ordered chili and talked obsessively of money. Rosen made the mistake of ordering meat loaf.

By the time they left the restaurant it had become dark. When they got back on the thruway the driver turned off the overhead light. Rosen leaned back in his seat, closed his eyes and listened to his stomach whine. After a time he slept and dreamt of Lila Bent who, laughing at something he said, blended with red-haired Ginny. He had been expounding on the emotional truth (that was the odd phrase) of "Ward 6" when Lila laughed, becoming Ginny...

Rosen, awake, monitored his stomach, then fell asleep again. By the time he was properly awake, it was past dawn and they were just west of Toledo.

The toilet went out in Kalamazoo and the bus smelled of it. Ginny and the infant blithely disembarked in Eau Claire, Wisconsin. A man with his right arm missing at the forearm boarded the bus and sat in Ginny's seat. He glared at Rosen with one lidless eye, not turning his head, saying nothing. That noon, at a lunch stop in Moorhead, Minnesota, the crippled man got into a conversation with the money-obsessed man in the yachting cap. Sitting a few tables away Rosen strained to overhear. The crippled man was named Hodge, had been a mess sergeant in the army, forcibly retired because of the arm which had been severed in a road accident near the base. This narrative Hodge bitterly related to his unwilling listener, who with less vitality could only make brief interjections: "What was your base pay then?...Hell, I was making a lot more than that...Do you have any idea what them Indy race car drivers make a race?...How about that Alley! Alley, the fighter. He's forty years old and just signed to fight for 20 million. Can you believe that!"

This last provoked in Hodge a sputtering diatribe on the subject of "niggers," which led after a time, predictably, to sex. Here Hodge leaned over the table, closed one eye, and lowered his voice, but his broad gestures and the occasional phrase indicated that he was boasting of his exceedingly virile, womb-disabling *stump*.

Back on the bus Hodge flashed Rosen a don't-fuck-with-me look through his baleful eye, deposited a fart, and fell stertorously asleep.

Hodge was still noisily asleep when a fatigued, dyspeptic Rosen got off at Miles City, Montana.

It was 11:20 a.m., cooler than Rosen expected for mid-September. The bus stop was on the strip leading into Miles City, and Rosen with his single canvas suitcase made his way past gas station, fast food restaurant, used car lot, and drive-in bank, walking at the side of the road. To the east were the eroded mesas and ridges of the Badlands; they seemed somehow frozen, immaterial. It took Rosen a wearying hour and a half to get to the small motel across from the railroad tracks. The rates were high; Rosen paid for a single night, went to his room and lay down on his back.

The humpback occupies his accustomed place in the wide grassy field. The sky is overcast, the wind is active. Rosen shouts the name "Aquinas!" as he throws his yellow ball high into the air. Aquinas does not move, the ball slants toward him as it descends, he catches it effortlessly. Margaret Fuller is next: she misses the ball. Then Lao-tse, who does not miss.

Rosen makes his notations.

Next he calls out the name "Lionel Bent!" and hurls the ball. Bent, seeming smaller than he is, visors his eyes with his hand, circling spasmodically. Evidently he cannot locate the ball. Suddenly—disregarding the ball's circuit—he turns his back and walks deliberately away. He takes out his mouth organ, commencing to play as he walks. Rosen (observing) notes with surprise that the receding Bent is not only quite small but oddly humped...

Awake, Rosen washed his hands and face, went out. It was past three, warmer. Rosen found his way to the "business loop," the typical agglomeration of industrial structures, shops, traffic, men in suits. He had not yet seen an identifiable Sioux. But then, drawing close to a rundown margin of the loop, he spotted two Indian men hunkering against a scrap of building, weeded over. They were squatting side-by-side. Rosen paused beside them.

"Hello."

One of the men nodded.

"I'm looking for someone," Rosen explained. "A large man with a beard who plays the mouth organ. The harmonica." Rosen mimed playing a harmonica. "Have you seen him?"

Neither of the men responded. Rosen stood there for a time but did not repeat the question.

"Thank you," he said and continued walking away from the business loop.

He saw a few other clusters of Indian men and paused at one where they were pitching bottle caps on the stony ground. He described Lionel Bent to one of the bystanders, who, even as Rosen was talking, shook his head no.

Rosen moved on. The area he was walking through was louse-poor; the sole "industry" the shacks that specialized in car-repair, body work, motorcycle repair; and an occasional rundown supplies store. Rosen stopped at one of these, bought a cup of coffee and a sweet roll, and asked the proprietor, an elderly Indian woman with clear black eyes, whether she had seen Bent. She listened attentively to his description, but finally shook her head.

"I am sorry. I do not know him."

"Thank you," Rosen smiled. He sipped his coffee at the counter, reluctant to leave. The old woman was a comforting presence. Her radiant eyes reminded him of Lila Bent's. Odd. She seemed as composed as Lila was mercurial, aberrant.

"Where do you come from?" she asked.

"Oh. I live in New York City."

"I see. And this other man, he also lives in New York?"

"He was living in New York. With his wife," Rosen said. "Then he left. He told his wife he was coming here, to Miles City."

"I see." The old woman smiled faintly. She didn't appear to think it unusual that someone would leave New York specifically for Miles City, Montana.

Another customer came into the store, Rosen said,

"Goodbye. Thank you."

She smiled again, a gentle, engaging smile, and waved her hand.

Rosen found his way back to the railroad tracks. Two black men and an Indian, dripping sweat in the deceptive sun, were repairing ties. Rosen approached them—but then changed his mind and returned to the motel. He sat on the bed and entered some sums into a notebook. He removed the Chekhov from his suitcase and began to read another story. But his eyes were tired, and he could not keep from thinking of Lionel. If he were playing his mouth organ and moving among the people, as he did in Maine and New York, why had none of those Rosen questioned seen him? On the opposite side of the business loop was a suburban living area which would be white. Bent would not be there. Rosen unfurled his map. Miles City was not large: the business loop, the white suburb to the north and northeast, the Indian ghetto to the south. Well, maybe he had not seen all of the Indian area. He would have a longer look tomorrow.

Rosen did not sleep well that night. The next morning he was on the move at 7:45. Since checkout time was not until noon, he left his suitcase at the motel. Again he followed the paved streets until they became cracked and weedy and gave way to dirt and stone. He made a point of investigating those side roads and paths he had not taken the day before. Few people were out. Three men almost in tandem, though separated by twenty or thirty meters, were evidently sleeping off drunks. The third motioned to Rosen, who walked up to him.

"You have smoke?"

Rosen said he didn't.

"I ain't workin, mister. You have twenty-five cent?"

Rosen handed him a quarter. He described Lionel Bent, and when the man seemed uncertain he showed him the photograph Lila had given him.

"I don't know," the man said, bringing the photo close to his face. It was then that Rosen saw that the man's eyes were so coated with film that iris and pupil were scarcely visible.

The man handed the photo back. "What you name?" he asked unexpectedly.

"Malcolm. And yours?"

"Elk Mole."

There was a silence.

Elk Mole said, "Why don't you go ask Cora? Bout this man you lookin for."

"Who is Cora?"

"Oh she own the store yonder." He pointed in the direction Rosen had been walking. "Cora know just bout everbody."

"What's the name of the store? Does it have a name?"

Elk Mole seemed momentarily puzzled. "Why, we just call it Cora's. Ain't but one Cora hereabout." Again he pointed.

"Okay. Thank you," Rosen said.

"See you round, Malcolm. Hey, Malcolm!"

Rosen turned around.

"What kind of music you friend play?"

"Mouth organ. Harmonica."

Elk Mole grinned. "Hell, Cora sell them things. In her store."

Rosen resumed walking. He recalled that one of the poems in Lionel's crate had alluded to a blind Indian. The poem had been called "Ute." That's all Rosen remembered about it. It was twenty past ten. Rosen asked two people on the street where Cora's store was, and both pointed approximately in the same direction. But still he didn't find it. Also he was now walking the same streets he had fruitlessly walked yesterday. He turned back.

In the motel he asked the woman in the office to put through a long distance call to Lila Bent in New York. Rosen heard the New York operator say that the number he requested—the number Lila had given to him before he left—was disconnected. When Rosen asked how long the number had been disconnected, and by whom, the operator said that her records merely indicated that the number was disconnected, nothing more.

Rosen put down the phone. He lay back on the bed with his hands behind his head. What could it be? Was Lila Bent having some elaborate fun at his expense? She was, he conceded, probably capable of doing such a thing. The more Rosen considered the more it seemed that Lila's story, eccentric as it was, had, as Raymond Chandler once put it, "the austere simplicity of fiction rather than the tangled woof of fact."

And yet Rosen believed her, believed that Lionel Bent had left and that Lila, in her peculiar way, was mourning his departure. Again he looked at the phone number in his notebook. He, not Lila, had written it down. It was possible he had gotten it wrong.

Rosen had the woman in the office dial the Miles City Public Library. The librarian said that the library did keep phone directories of certain cities, including New York, but that they were short-handed, Rosen would have to look through the directory himself. He thanked her.

The librarian's directions, which Rosen checked against his map, indicated that the library was not in or near the business loop but in the Indian area from which he had just returned. So far as he could tell from the map, he must have passed the library that same morning, without noticing it.

It was nearly noon. Not expecting to spend another night in the motel, he packed his suitcase, strapped it across his back and set off once again into the Sioux ghetto.

The suitcase felt awkward and heavy across his narrow shoulders, and he was tired. The frustration, the accumulated lack of sleep on the long bus ride, the weight on his back—all of these had made him bone weary. And yet he wasn't precisely uncomfortable. Strange to say, he felt emptied and alert. In fact, walking—for the third time in two days—into the Indian area, it was as though he had not seen it before. The irregular contours of the wooden shacks against the white birch and mountain ash were reflected in the looming mesas and ridges, browns and tans, under a blue-white sky. Threadbare Indians occupied the streets, walking, squatting, riding bicycles or mules, carrying heavy parcels on their backs. Rosen walked among them, sometimes catching an eye, sometimes nodding.

Instead of asking directions to the library, Rosen used his map. He was following it back to where he had spoken with the blind man—who was no longer there—in the direction the blind man had pointed. Rosen walked deliberately, even lightly, despite his burden. At one point he picked up a peeled branch from the ground, which he used as a walking stick and to keep the unruly dogs at bay.

Passing through a dusty area where several Indian children were playing, one boy pointed at Rosen's back and said, "hump." He said this matter-of-factly, as he might have said "nose" or "crow." Hump, Rosen remembered, was a Sioux chief mentioned in some of Lionel's poems.

Rosen paused, consulted his map; the library would have to be close by. Then he saw the supplies store, where he had spoken with the old woman. He could ask her.

She was sitting on a high stool behind the counter.

"Hello," she said, smiling in her graceful way.

Rosen had forgotten her smile.

A woman with her young son in tow walked to the counter from the back of the store carrying a small wooden flute.

She said, "How much is this one, Cora?"

The lady behind the counter—Cora—said a price, wrapped the flute in brown paper and handed it back. She turned to Rosen.

"And have you found your friend? What was his name?"

"Bent," Rosen said. "Lionel Bent. No, I haven't found him." He paused.

Cora was regarding him with her radiant black eyes.

"You sell," Rosen asked, "musical instruments?"

"Yes," she laughed softly. "Have a look, in the back."

In the back of the store, sharing a low shelf with alfalfa hay and bone meal and fertilizer were three harmonicas. Rosen picked one up and placed it to his lips...

To the east are the mesas and ridges of the Badlands, browns and tans, beneath a gold high sun. To the west: the sheer face of cliff, snow-tipped crag, chasm. Between, on the grassy plain, humped Rosen with his yellow ball. He hurls it high effortlessly, and as it sails up and up beyond cloud, beyond sight, Rosen lowers his head, removes the small mouth organ from his canvas suitcase and produces a single high echoing note...

FICTION COLLECTIVE
Books in Print

Order from Flatiron Book Distributors Inc., 175 Fifth Avenue NYC 10010